CW00347834

VOICES FROM THE NORTH

New writing from Norway

VOICES FROM THE NORTH
New writing from Norway

Edited by
Vigdis Ofte & Steinar Sivertsen

MAIA

Published in 2008 by
The Maia Press Limited
82 Forest Road
London E8 3BH
www.maiapress.com

Steinar Sivertsen, introduction © Steinar Sivertsen 2008, translated by John Irons

Kjartan Fløgstad, essay © Kjartan Fløgstad 2008, translation © James Anderson 2008

Johan Harstad, short stories from *Ambulanse*, © Gyldendal Norsk Forlag 2002, translated by Deborah Dawkin and Erik Skuggevik

Einar O. Risa, extracts from *Kom, kom, hør nattergalen*, © Tiden Norsk Forlag 2005, and *Jeg går ikke ut, jeg svever over byen*, © Tiden Norsk Forlag 2006, translated by Ren Powell

Øyvind Rimbereid, poems from *Seine topografiar*, © Gyldendal Norsk Forlag 2000; *Solaris korrigert*, © Gyldendal Norsk Forlag 2004, and short story from *Kommende År*, © Gyldendal Norsk Forlag 1998, translated by John Irons

For foreign rights please contact Gyldendal Agency / eva.lie-nielsen@gyldendal.no

Tore Renberg, extracts from *Kompani Orheim*, © Forlaget Oktober 2005, translated by Don Bartlett

Sigmund Jensen, extracts from *Hvite dverger. Svarte hull*, © Aschehoug Forlag 2002, translated by May-Brit Akerholt

Torild Wardenær, poems from *Titanporten*, © Aschehoug Forlag 2001; *Paradiseffekten*, © Aschehoug Forlag 2004, and *psi*, 2007, translated by John Irons

For foreign rights please contact Aschehoug Agency, PO Box 363 Sentrum, NO-0102 Oslo, Norway / epost@aschehougagency.no

All rights reserved. No part of this publication may be reproduced, stored in a retrieval system, or transmitted in any form or by any means, electronic, mechanical, photocopying, recording or otherwise, without the prior written permission of the publisher, nor be otherwise circulated in any form of binding or cover other than that in which it is published and without a similar condition including this condition being imposed on the subsequent publisher

ISBN 978 1 904559 29 0

A CIP catalogue record for this book is available from the British Library

Printed and bound in Great Britain by Thanet Press on paper from sustainable managed forests

This edition is supported by NORLA (Norwegian Literature Abroad)  N O R L A

The Maia Press is supported by Arts Council England

STAVANGER
2008
EUROPEAN CAPITAL
OF CULTURE

Main sponsors

TOTAL

Stavanger Aftenblad

Spare Bank 1
SR-Bank

Lyse

With this book
Stavanger2008 aims to give
authors from Rogaland in
Norway the chance to be
read in the English-language
book market. Rogaland has
fostered many great authors,
and the 1990s in particular
was a long golden age for the
region, during which all the
writers included here
published their first works.

CONTENTS

VIA THE LOCAL TO THE GLOBAL
Steinar Sivertsen

In his essay 'Tradition and the Individual Talent', T. S. Eliot stresses that the significance of a poet's work can never be fully appreciated in isolation. 'You cannot value him alone,' writes Eliot. 'You must set him, for contrast and comparison, among the dead.'

The seven prize-winning writers contributing their work to this anthology also exist in a concrete historical and social context, against a particular literary background. They made their literary debuts at different points in time and thus belong to different generations of writers, although all of them have a connection with Stavanger and Rogaland County. All of the writers featured here have had a university education and possess a written voice that challenges the language of the media, communicating alternative, contrary images of reality. Most of them have had work translated into foreign languages and many collaborate frequently with artists and musicians. Some have written epic texts that have been dramatised or turned into films, and all of them adopt a conscious stance on both tradition and contemporary literature – local, national and

VOICES FROM THE NORTH | STAVANGER2008

global. Not unexpectedly, a number of these writers have been inspired by the three most central classic writers of the region – the 'Jærbu' (i.e. from the coastal area of Jæren) and European Arne Garborg (1851–1924); the realistic short-story writer, novelist and social agitator Alexander L. Kielland (1849–1906), and the neo-romantic modernist Sigbjørn Obstfelder (1866–1900). For a long time, the literary community of Rogaland comprised relatively few members. This has changed. During the 1990s, so many writers from Stavanger and the local area published debut works that the head of the Writers' Union of Norway was asked to comment on the sudden upsurge of literary activity. He explained that work to strengthen the position of literature in public consciousness had been ongoing for a number of years in Stavanger and elsewhere in the county. Ambitious cultural plans, frequent literary events, activities in libraries and schools, combined with increased coverage in local newspapers and commercial sponsorship – all of this means that the literary infrastructure is particularly well developed in the region.

KJARTAN FLØGSTAD

Many aggressive, unhappy writers have made protest against the environment of their childhood an artistic caste mark. The most prominent representative of today's Rogaland literature, Kjartan Fløgstad, does the opposite. Born in 1944 in the small industrial location of Sauda in Ryfylke (the inner island and fjord settlements in Rogaland County), Fløgstad has a deep affiliation with his own social roots and the culture that developed around the local foundry and Folkets Hus (People's House), its landscape and waterfront. Writing in neo-Norwegian (*nynorsk*) – a minority language which is, officially, on a par with the predominant language, *bokmål* – he has published over forty books in various genres. The most important precondition for his writing is the melting pot of Sauda, created by the hard work, laughter and dreams of generations.

More consistently than any other contemporary Norwegian writer, Fløgstad has shed light on capitalism, working-class culture and the welfare state from the inside. In his educated, elegant fashion, he launches a sledgehammer attack on the academic authorities who devalue the popular language of neo-Norwegian and distort the history of language in Norway. With a profusion of factual material, he reveals how Oslo has become a de-industrialised city in which alienated producers of ideologies refuse to realise that it is the vitality of regional and oil-producing Norway that keeps the capital alive. Fløgstad consistently speaks with exemplary weight on behalf of an area on the socio-geographical fringe from which he has never wished to disassociate himself.

This does not imply that Fløgstad is a stay-at-home who has remained within restricted circles. After completing his secondary education, he roamed wide both in life and literature. Among other things, Fløgstad can look back on discontinued studies as an architect and a philologist. He has worked in Sauda's cornerstone industry, the Electric Furnace Products Company, owned by Union Carbide, and as a greaser on merchant ships. This well-spoken, prize-winning and frequently translated writer is always on the move as an ambassador for literary Norway – an aspect of his life reflected in both his novels and travel books.

Fløgstad's debut as a writer took place in 1968, with a collection of postmodern poetry, *Valfart* (Pilgrimage), in which he made his appearance as a *poeta doctus*, a well-read, aesthetically oriented poet without any leanings towards politically committed literature. The collection also included translations of Jacobean poets such as John Marston, John Webster and Cyril Tourneur.

Fangliner (Painters, 1971), a rough collection of short stories with titles related to shipping, marked a profound change in the nature of Fløgstad's authorship. In a neo-Norwegian indicating distrust of the traditional 'literary' dialect, he depicted characters representative of various social strata, especially workers and seamen. In a short space of time, industrial work, in the form of concrete actions and everyday routines, became a major motif in his writing. From this point on he was no longer interested in content or in form, but rather in the relationships between the two.

Fløgstad has commented on his change in literary direction in a number of highly erudite essay collections, including *Loven vest for Pecos* (The law west of Pecos, 1981). In this he dealt with cultural industry and industrial working-class culture, praising socially degraded art forms such as B-movies, hard-boiled detective stories and rock music, which he considered to be arenas in which subversion was still possible. It is popular culture, not high art, which now offers resistance to today's totalitarian media society and a highbrow culture that unfolds in bourgeois settings, on stages and in concert halls, in privileged, cultivated and enervated form. Refusing to use the predominant language of *bokmål*, Fløgstad prefers the counterforce of the proletarian dialect he learned in the iron-alloy foundry in Sauda. Instead of aiming for heroic social realism, he looks to pop culture and a fantastic realism which has its roots in the baroque and the surreal.

These elements, which distinguish Fløgstad's essays, are also to be found in his novels. He has repeatedly stated that through the esoteric and the theoretical lies the way to the local and popular – to an impure, wild prose that rollercoasters between highs and lows. When hitchhiking around South America in 1970 he became familiar with Latin-American magic realism in such writers as Cortazár, Borges and Márquez. At the same time, he read the Russian literary researcher Bakhtin, in whose opinion popular art in industrial society is a continuation of the carnival tradition in the feudal state. Fløgstad believes that only in becoming alchemists of style and genre, breaking down the established division between everyday language, elevated language and low prose, can modern writers create the complex, grotesque realism that includes the inheritance of Lucian, Menippean satire and Rabelais, and undermine the cultural hegemony of those in power. The aim is to create pulsating, polyphonic hybrid texts that are accessible to people other than the academically blasé. From such a perspective, Raymond Chandler,

Clint Eastwood and Elvis Presley become more important than Henrik Ibsen and Knut Hamsun. In the mid-1970s, Fløgstad wrote two hard-boiled detective novels under a pseudonym.

However, more central to his work are the novels *Rasmus* (1974), *Dalen Portland* (1978; translated as *Dollar Road*, 1989) and *Fyr og flamme* (Fire and flames, 1980). Here, he reveals how old Norwegian farming society was reformed into a modern industrial state, and how new production conditions gave rise to new lifestyles and value systems. The fiction spreads out, fan-shaped, through space and time, from the foundry in Ryfylke to the jungle of Latin America, but the imaginative force behind it is held in check by the seriousness of Marxism. The result is a sensitive, exuberant piece of working-class literature that avoids the false proletarian folklorism typical of a number of left-wing, socially realistic novels in Norwegian literature of the 1970s. Fløgstad gained the literary award of the Nordic Council for *Dalen Portland* and the Literary Critics' Prize for *Fyr og Flamme*, an indication of the encyclopaedic range and linguistic diversity that have made him perhaps the most prestigious contemporary writer in Norway.

In a decade when political writing was no longer in fashion, Fløgstad wrote *U3* (1983), a protest against Norwegian defence policy and NATO's role in the Cold War. His massive novel *Det syvende klima* (The seventh climate, 1986) is an intricate showdown between the writer and a banal commercial media society. It is also a tribute to the vital 'fringe' art that pushes against the rules of good form by adorning, distorting and innovating. Both *Kniven på strupen* (The knife at one's throat, 1991) and *Fimbul* (1994) are contemporary social satirical novels with traits of the detective story. Also worth mentioning is *Kron og mynt. Eit veddemål* (Heads or tails. A wager, 1998), a kaleidoscopic baroque novel for our time which, at 500-plus pages, is the writer's most comprehensive work. The geographical centre of gravity in this work lies in Stavanger and the surrounding area, but in typical Fløgstad fashion the plot shifts out into the world, and the massive wave of writing sweeps swiftly through a wide range of motifs.

In *Paradis på jord* (Paradise on earth, 2002), Fløgstad combines a road movie with a journey of political education. A Chilean with an indigenous mother travels north in search of his Norwegian father's family. With a wry look at Chilean history, Western imperialism and the prejudices of wealthy Norway, and an interest in the nomadic existence of the refugee, Americanisation and the problems of globalisation, Fløgstad the fabulist has written his most accessible novel.

Interwoven e-mails and metrical poems make *Grand Manila* (2007) one of Fløgstad's star turns. With industrial workers from Lovra (a fictionalised version of Sauda) as its point of departure, the novel is topical in its depiction of globalisation and an increasingly market-dictated world. The solidarity of the proletariat of the past at a factory in Ryfylke is linked to a suicide in the wake of the Finnish civil war. *Grand Manila* is concerned not only with the increasing importance of the state, but also the mass murder that Union Carbide has been responsible for on three continents – not only in Arundhati Roy's Bhopal, but also in West Virginia and Sauda. At the same time, the writer's scepticism regarding elitist modernism and institutionalised art come to the fore. The anonymous narrator in the novel prefers American bluegrass and Finnish tango (i.e. popular music) to highbrow masterpieces. A classically educated singer gives up her career, leaving the bourgeois salon behind to become a travelling singer at weddings, pondering 'how good bad art can be. And how bad good art.'

Historian and avant-garde fabulist, a man who has translated Pablo Neruda into neo-Norwegian, Fløgstad, like Neruda himself, knows that 'the one who runs from bad taste will slip on the ice'. Fløgstad has never sought to prompt unanimous applause, insisting instead that his novels prompt dialogue and offer resistance.

The cultural pessimist Adorno was wrong. The novel is not an extinct genre. The world lives in the anti-totalitarian, dissonant language of the writer. Like Brecht, Fløgstad acknowledges: 'Kunst ist nichts Individuelles. Kunst ist, sowohl was ihre Entstehung als auch ihre Wirkung betrifft, etwas Kollektives.' (Art is not something individual. Art, as regards both its origin and its effect, is something collective.) His aesthetic ideal is identical with what Roland Barthes has referred to as gongoristic texts: 'texts where the richness of the language can be fully exploited, in all the double and treble meanings of the word, and at all linguistic levels, with overtones of all kinds of technical language, language for specific purposes, dialect and jargon.' Not until then, by transforming one's experiences, thoughts, emotions and fantasies into the labyrinths of fiction, and arriving at a form of writing that goes against the tabloid powerprose of the media, does the writer master something no scientist can attain in his objective approach to the world – allowing the noise and the hot breath from a thousand voices to bring forth a utopian, transcending element, so that 'What we invent will become/Truer than experience!' (*Dalen Portland*).

JOHAN HARSTAD

Johan Harstad, born in Stavanger in 1979, made his debut with a collection of short prose pieces *Herfra blir du bare eldre* (From here on you just get older, 2001). The 52 untitled texts in the collection range from just a few lines to four pages long. The tone is melancholy, disillusioned, devoid of irony, reminiscent of David Coupland's *Generation X*. Themes of pain, sorrow and resignation, often the result of loneliness, war or death, are transmitted from text to text like distorted radio signals. The oppressive awareness that 'from now on you'll only get older' thuds between the lines in which memories of certain formative experiences emerge. Sensory impressions and dreamlike fantasies reveal the striking distance between the multitude of fictive, anonymous narrators and the world they inhabit. But a ray of light shines through the darkness. The certainty that children continue to be born causes the feelings of alienation, loss and despondency to die down, and a lovely incident burns itself into the memory, 'a unique mental image of the moment where the world is good'. On rare occasions, the all-pervasive loneliness is transcended: 'Behind me I can hear that she is asleep. Her breathing is calm, regular.'

The book was well received, and praised for the stylistic assurance of the writer as well his unsentimental confrontation with a harsh reality. But more rigorous editing was recommended, since many of the shortest texts seemed to be loose ideas, swift flashes of thought.

This criticism could not be levelled at the author's next work: the collection of short stories *Ambulanse* (Ambulance, 2002). These eleven well-constructed pieces have so great an inner cohesion that the collection could be termed a 'short-story-novel'. For these are tales that wave and whisper to each other, not only because one senses their common interest in the basic conditions of existence, but also because some of the same characters and certain leitmotifs – such as the ambulance – echo from short to story, binding the material together. Harstad has said that this filmic montage technique was inspired by the Polish writer and director, Krzysztof Kieslowski.

The characters in *Ambulanse* are often in vulnerable positions. Disaster looms, an existential disquiet persists, social patterns prompt behaviour that seems absurd. At the same time, there seems to be a greater willingness to resist suffering, even when it is self-inflicted, than was the case in Harstad's first book. '113', the title of the opening short story, for example, refers to the emergency telephone number in Norway, suggesting that help is accessible and survival possible. The urban existence we are familiar with is problematic enough, but not hopeless. One can change one's everyday life. Ambulances go to and fro. Proximity is possible. Love exists.

A central motif in contemporary Norwegian literature is the individual in a state of mental imbalance or existential vacuum, who drops out of the Norwegian welfare state. An example of this kind of breakdown and breakout story is Harstad's novel, *Buzz Aldrin, hvor ble det av deg i alt mylderet?* (Buzz Aldrin, what happened to you in all the confusion?, 2005). Painted with a broad brush, the author refers to Robert Creeley's words: 'What did I know/thinking myself/able to go/alone all the way.' Set in 2019, Mattias, the novel's protagonist, tells us of his childhood and youth, his mental crises and the adult life that for a long time threatens to capsize. This is a shut-up-and-back-to-everyday-life story that shows us our need to be loved, the value of being a second child and almost invisible, the joy that binds days together, and the pain when death suddenly happens. Written in four parts, each part titled with the name of a song by the Swedish pop band Cardigans, the book is 633 pages long. The words are thoughtful and heartfelt.

Mattias was born in 1969, the same day that Buzz Aldrin left the moon landing-craft *Eagle* and became the second man to set foot on the Sea of Tranquillity. That Buzz Aldrin – overshadowed by the heroic Neil Armstrong and quickly forgotten – becomes the prime object of the narrator's childhood fascination reflects Mattias's desire not to become a winner. He aims for the anonymous, an existence beyond fame and honour, a peaceful everyday life, protected and in the background. But at the age of thirty, after two routine, peaceful years with his partner, Mattias, a nurseryman from Stavanger, has an encounter with destiny. His partner leaves him, he loses his job and travels to the Faroe Islands with some musician friends. There he has a breakdown. From 1999 to 2002 he is in a psychiatric treatment centre. Alongside the skewed souls of the other residents, he learns how to tackle loss, sorrow and longing, eventually leaving the Faroese landscape in a home-made boat, setting sail for the Caribbean island of Grenada. The story is touching in all its self-effacing slowness. Once again, the reader is reminded of an important, indeed essential, fact: man is not alone on this earth and must never abandon hope of being able to give and to receive love. This feel-good story was highly praised by critics and has been translated into a number of languages. Its appeal is easy to understand: here we have a young author who, without irony, writes exemplary, generous prose. With the courage to undertake necessary detours and to linger at the apparently undramatic, Harstad lives up to Franz Kafka's claim that 'a book must be the axe for the frozen sea within us.'

TORE RENBERG

Tore Renberg, born in 1972, received the debut writing prize for *Søvende floke* (Sleeping tangle, 1995), a compact collection of short prose works in which the author, in a slightly intellectual, academic spirit, allows 72 untitled pieces of various lengths to converse with each other – about life, death and love, bodily signals, the secrets of the memory, the challenges of thought. Much of it is keenly sensed and intelligently constructed.

Within a short space of time, Renberg has made his mark as a fearless 'rock' version of classical Renaissance man – an artist who, with violent energy, expresses himself within various fields and is always prepared to take on new public roles. The novel *Matriarkat* (Matriarchy, 1996) enters into a dialogue with cultural leftists and feminists by focusing on various sex roles in the light of the crisis-hit nuclear family. The 23-year-old narrator loves his young 'mamma', is fascinated by his little sister, has an alcoholic father and a shaky sexual identity. With his outré depiction of masculine sexuality and personality formation, centred on the portrait of an overgrown boy who lives through women and for women, the book gave rise to a lively debate.

The title of Renberg's next book, *Mamma, pappa, barn* (Mummy, daddy, children, 1997) was taken from a Swedish punk band, and says something about the author's choice of themes and his attitude. Via sprawling, often rough, prose texts, through many allusions, he adopts the role of provocateur and writes 'verbal punk' – a hornet's nest of intersecting ideas and tirades, where sex, longing, shame, grief, happiness and God are at the centre.

In the 1890s, the writings of social struggle made way for more religiously tinged literature, something that is reflected in the novel *Fred* (Peace) by Arne Garborg, a work cited on the last page of *Mamma, pappa, barn*. The same metaphysical orientation was to be found in Norwegian writers at the turn of the millennium. The shocking contemporary novel *Renselse* (Purification, 1998) is, for example, a Passion about religious longing that gets out of control, as is the case in *Fred*. The first-person narrator is an epileptic, Jakob

Malde, who wants to do what is good, but does what is evil. With considerable rhetorical power, inspired by Garborg, and with echoes too of Ibsen, Kierkegaard, Dostoievsky and the Book of Genesis, Renberg writes in a beautiful, wild and high-flown prophetic language. Here, the biblical story of Jacob's struggle is rewritten with a tragic outcome, before the word is given to God himself.

A god tid (A good time, 2000), with its subtitle 'Memories of the future', is described as 'A love story from a time that is to come, in memory of the time that has been.' The novel is a depiction of the world at the end of the twentieth century, written in the style of a science-fiction story penned decades earlier. Indeed, the text claims that it was written in 1925–26 by an unsuccessful writer named Tore Renberg, born in 1898 in Stavanger.

The coming-of-age novel *Mannen som elsket Yngve* (The man who loved Yngve, 2003) marks a watershed in Renberg's writing. Here, he works with breadth and realism, through a first-person narrator whose character is reminiscent of the writer himself. With pulsating enthusiasm the novel follows the lives of a group of young men from Stavanger who become adults against the backdrop of the fall of the Berlin Wall. Full of energy, this turbo-charged, locally based story also has a wider resonance. Set in 2003, the narrative voice belongs to 30-year-old Jarle Klepp who, with immediacy and fire, recalls life when he was 17 and a singer in a rock band. Renberg's accustomed investigation of gender roles is reflected in the surprising story of the rebellious narrator who, although previously heterosexual, falls hopelessly in love with a gay tennis-playing fellow-pupil at the town's grammar school. Like Marcel Proust (surely one of Renberg's literary household gods), Renberg is in search of lost time, and he unfolds and shakes out the social, political, cultural and sexual experiences that coloured the life of a whole generation. This results in a highly accessible page-turner which generated enthusiastic criticism and sales, translation into various languages and which is now set to become a full-length feature film.

From his innovative, intellectual debut work to the psychological realism of *Mannen som elsket Yngve*, Renberg has consistently displayed a strong desire to vary his modes of literary expression. This is also reflected in his prize-winning novel *Kompani Orheim* (The Orheim Company, 2005), which continues the story about Jarle and Yngve. Renberg's style and choice of a third-person, omniscient narrator suggest that realists such as Kielland, Balzac and Dickens have now become his most important literary influences. The use of melodramatic elements encouraged by such classic writers is far more visible in *Kompani Orheim* than the avant-garde techniques employed in Renberg's early books. Although the framing narrative is set in 1996, when the main character, Jarle Klepp, is studying in Bergen and hears that his father has died, the novel is primarily concerned with Jarle's formative years in a middle-class Stavanger home during the 1970s and 1980s. More than any of his earlier works, *Kompani Orheim* displays Renberg's capacity for empathy. The characters dredge their hearts of old ashes and find reasons for living – without concealing the rifts in their souls or denying their harmonised disharmonies.

Renberg belongs to a generation writing in the ruins of the collapsed nuclear family. With an urban, youthful language that carries its own pulse, he manages to convey how a young man can live through what is unnameable: alcoholism, fear, domestic abuse – experiences that create invisible tattoos on his soul, traumas that can never completely be erased. But Renberg is no pitch-black pessimist raking around in well-mined misery. The protagonist embraces his mother with such warmth that one can literally feel the heartstrings woven into the text. He praises friendship with political fervour. He laughs at adolescent infatuation and wildness, takes pleasure in music, books and films, has a zest for life and a drive that is infectious.

In 2006 Renberg published a 'double novel': *Farmor har kabel-TV* (Grandma's got cable TV) and *Videogutten* (The video boy), two texts that contrast and complement each other. The first story is warm and melancholy, dealing with two teenagers who visit one of their grandmothers to watch music videos on Sky TV. More sombre in tone and laden with symbolism is the second story, of two 14-year-olds who go off to an unfamiliar part of town to see uncensored splatter videos. Once again, Renberg connects with a tradition that goes back to the small-town chronicler Kielland, reshaping his own experiences as a young man into writing that is deeply credible in its psychological realism.

SIGMUND JENSEN
Sigmund Jensen, born in 1968, made his debut with *Antikvarens datter og andre noveller* (The Antiquarian's daughter and other stories) in 1995. This is a collection of a dozen stories, most of them misanthropic and critical of society; however, Jensen does not portray existence as completely hopeless. After the narrator has related a stream of new, gloomy glimpses into the lives of people of both sexes and various ages at times of crisis, the collection is rounded off by the title story – a beautiful, optimistic reminder that change, love and poetic magic, despite all, are still possible.

In his precise, minimal style, Jensen writes about domestic abuse, fear, meaninglessness, the incapacity to deal with life, financial difficulties, difficult births, mental distress, self-harm, passivity, egocentricity, breakdown of communication, existential pain and death. His expressive, repetitive prose can sometimes seem very insistent – Jensen is no aloof modernist scrabbling for a subtext. He is a learned chronicler who renders detailed backdrops against which characters comment on their own or other people's miseries.

Built into these fin-de-siècle texts, often set in Stavanger, is an avalanche of quotations and allusions, especially to literature, philosophy, films and music. A key influence is Samuel Beckett, although Kierkegaard, Nietzsche, Schopenhauer and Camus should also be mentioned – classical observers of the loss of meaning and melancholy reflected in these acrid, well-constructed short stories.

The stylistic and thematic relationship to Jensen's next book *Motvilje* (Antipathy, 1998) is obvious. In eight stories, full of allusions and told from various perspectives, he once again introduces individuals who, in various social contexts, strive to achieve a meaningful existence. But the dialogues are more frequent and the monologue less pronounced than in the author's debut work. Sardonic humour and the poking of gentle fun at human folly and existential conditions are a recurrent feature.

The high point of Jensen's work to date is his extremely ambitious novel *Hvite dverger. Svarte hull* (White dwarves. Black holes, 2002), an all-inclusive project of just over 450 pages, in which he draws on much of what he has experienced and read and learned: the result is a novel with a striking richness of language and an encyclopaedic span. The title stretches a universe over a textual framework and can be interpreted symbolically: a white dwarf is an astronomical concept that refers to a dying star; a black hole is the grave of a star. Thus the title introduces the sombre keynote of the novel as a whole. It deals with a barbaric civilisation that is undermining itself, populated with a people who are in the process of committing suicide through wars, squandered resources and other fatal symptoms of decline. The novel debates the grotesque prosperity of the West when compared to the poverty of the rest of the world, portraying Western society as a capitalist, neo-cannibalistic world order which does not deserve to survive.

In sections set in the present day, printed in italics, the author describes a psychiatric institution. There, the first-person narrator, a 33-year-old English stockbroker named Gestas Hutting, reflects on his flaky life of financial embezzlement, drug abuse and collapsed relationships. In the aftermath of his father's death, and with Scotland Yard on his heels, this representative of the former imperial power flees to India, and it is this twisting, dramatic journey from Madras to Varanasi, via Calcutta and along the Ganges, that forms the basic framework of the novel.

Through encounters with the countryside and other people travelling through it, with the aid of overt or covert quotations, symbolism, essayistic snapshots and a whole host of allusions, Jensen creates an elegantly interwoven text that fans out over the

geography of landscape and ideas. Poetic sensibility, a broad historical panorama, an analysis of contemporary politics, a dive into
philosophy, metaphysical musings, a touch of cultural satire, discussions about religion and the history of ideas, academic insight,
baroque entanglements, existential seriousness, irony and black
humour – all are present in this book.

Just as Dante, in 99 cantos, takes the reader through 'Inferno' and
'Purgatorio' to 'Paradiso', in *Hvite dverger. Svarte hull* Jensen uses
99 chapters to depict the main character's pilgrimage towards self-
knowledge. His name (Gestas) and his age (33) link the text to the
story of Christ's sufferings and the crucified robber who chose
perdition instead of salvation, while the 'Magdalen Mental Mercy-
seat', where our trauma-ridden traveller through India finally lands
up, is a reference to Beckett's novel *Murphy*, listed in the epilogue as
one of 31 books (many by English-language authors) that provided
source material for this unusually reference-rich novel. Better than
most, Sigmund Jensen demonstrates the truth of T. S. Eliot's assertion: 'The minor poet borrows; the major poet steals.'

The symbolic title of the short story collection *Gammaglimt*
(Gamma glimpse, 2004) also refers to astronomy and the cosmos,
more precisely to the radiance emitted when a star dies. All the
pieces in the book contain echoes of the insight that finds expression
in the opening story: 'Death is a gamma ray burst. Just a little
flicker.' The opening and concluding stories are dystopias. Stavanger
and the rest of the world are portrayed as a war zone, an inferno of
fear and violence, noise, loneliness and cries of pain. With these two
dark visions of the future as a frame for the seven stories anchored in
the present, Jensen, in his role as prophet of doom, continues his
project of criticising civilisation.

But despite the fact that the crisis-ridden characters feel power-
less, even though alienation survives and death threatens, towards
the end of the novel the reader encounters another doomsday
prophet, crying with one eye and winking with the other. The book
ends in an image redolent of both dark and light: 'On every street
corner a new girl pregnant with more suffering – and more summer.'

EINAR O. RISA

In 1995, several Stavanger writers published debut works – among them the cultural journalist Einar O. Risa, born in 1954, with the novel *Skygger* (Shadows). The action takes place in the Polish city of Wroclaw, after the fall of Communism. The narrator is an entrepreneur who, in an intense, suggestive, first-person narrative, talks about the difficulties involved in starting a tabloid newspaper and a publishing firm based on a Western, profit-oriented model. The title and the fragmentary plot imply the impossibility of escaping either your own shadow or history. The prose is rhythmic and hectic, the syntax characterised by long sentences and repetitions.

The action in Risa's first-person novel *Ring* (1996) takes place partly in a densely populated area of Norway, partly in Frankfurt during the annual Book Fair. With a satirical grin, the nervy, pulsating monologue follows a lovesick history teacher from Stavanger. The title can be interpreted in many ways, alluding to both the circular composition and the protagonist's desire for the telephone to ring.

Velvære (Well-being, 1997) is about ethnic cleansing in eastern Poland. Set in 1942, the novel gradually establishes its characters: twelve German soldiers, an officer and his wife. Risa's focus here is on the individual choices and urges that lie behind the official history syllabus. With allusions to Joseph Conrad's *Heart of Darkness* and the French Revolution, Risa creates an intense, staccato prose that shifts in focus between the Holocaust and the present day, the trivial and the monstrous.

In *Nasjonaldagen* (Independence Day, 1998), Risa looks at seduction and deceit in relation to the dissolution of the union between Norway and Sweden in 1905. Through a dramatic love triangle, he demonstrates how common people become pawns in political games they are unable to avoid or uncover. In language that seems less fragmentary than that of his earlier works, the novel demonstrates how a love affair can be sacrificed to national interests and an individual can become a tragic walk-on figure in his or her own life.

Nasjonaldagen, like *Velvære* and Risa's next novel *Helvete* (Hell, 1999) all make reference to the work of Joseph Conrad. *Helvete* also alludes to the film *Apocalypse Now* and, perhaps more importantly, Dante's *Divine Comedy*. In *Helvete*, however, the protagonist does not reach paradise. He is a refugee who ends up in the hell for asylum seekers – Norway.

Mannen i speilet (The man in the mirror, 1999) is a fictionalised biography of Alexander L. Kielland, the first of Risa's most recent 'biographical novels' in which he demonstrates an awareness that what he writes is a particular version of a life and that the definitive biography can never be written.

In the semi-documentary prize-winning *L. C. Nielsens papirer* (L. C. Nielsen's papers, 2000), Risa created a portrait of Sigbjørn Obstfelder, a 'poète maudit' who roamed restlessly through life; a literary dissident in exile who is said to have been the model for the main character in Rilke's *Malte Laurids Brigge*, and who was more famous in Vienna than in his home town of Stavanger. Risa conjures an image of an exemplary modernist juggling themes such as home-lessness, alienation and the fragmentation of the self.

Risa's next novel won even greater critical attention. *Casanovas siste erobring* (Casanova's last conquest, 2002) is narrated by the legendary seducer himself, and invites the reader into eighteenth-century Europe, at a period when the aristocracy ruled and the threat of revolution was in the air. At over 600 pages, written as a retrospective monologue by the ageing Giacomo Casanova (1725–98), this is Risa's most comprehensive work.

In the novel *Likeså, skulle han si* (Likewise, he would say, 2003), the author again sends fictitious characters out into the world to various European cities, while gradually zooming in on a soul in crisis. The action refers back to *Helvete* of 1999, taking as its subject the tragic life story of a high court judge.

Kom, kom, hør nattergalen (Come, come, listen to the nightin-gale, 2005) is a biographical novel about the Stavanger-born artist Peder Severin Krøyer (1851–1909), believed by his contemporaries to be the foremost painter in Scandinavia, but unable to change his egocentric way of life. In a rhythmically distinctive prose style, the contrast is revealed between the light summer mood of the painter's Impressionistic pictures from the idyll of Skagen in Denmark and the many conflicts with which the syphilitic, manic-depressive artist had to wrestle. In a brief framed story set at the 1909 Venice Biennale, a futuristic art critic takes delight in massacring Krøyer's pictures – labelling him an ageing, reactionary sketcher out of tune with the spirit of the age. Risa then sets out the story of Krøyer's life: the lad from Stavanger who did not know who his father was, who ended up with foster parents in Copenhagen, made a career, got married and then divorced from the beautiful, gifted painter Marie – a man who almost went blind and who tragically repressed the thought of anything that threatened his family's happiness.

Jeg går ikke ut lenger, jeg svever over byen (I don't go out any longer, I hover above the town, 2006) follows the friendship between the first-person narrator, an unnamed journalist from Stavanger, and a professor of Norwegian literature in Copenhagen. The action moves between a number of European cities and time zones, and touches on illness, drugs and erotic love. Pausing also to consider certain paintings or books, Risa is frequently concerned with the problem of interpretation and art.

ØYVIND RIMBEREID

Among the new voices of Rogaland literature to emerge in the 1990s was Øyvind Rimbereid, born in Stavanger in 1966. He made his debut in 1993 with a short story collection, *Det har begynt* (It has begun) – eleven pieces founded in realism and enigma. Norwegian critics unanimously confirmed Rimbereid as a technically skilful minimalist who had mastered the arts of both allusion and precision.

In an essay, Rimbereid refers to Goethe's assertion that the short story revolves around an 'unheard-of event'. Most of the main characters in his collection experience moments that cause a fissure in their everyday lives. Quivering with aggression, struggling for certainty or resolution, his characters are unreconciled with the realities of their own lives and fumbling for some sort of change. At first glance, the author seems to take relatively undramatic scenes as points of departure, but the writing never becomes flat or unambiguous. These are intense, disturbing stories filled with moments of illumination and obscurity. While conveying powerful sensory experiences and dialogues, each contains something unknown, unresolved, unsaid.

Thematically, Rimbereid belongs to a classical modernist tradition, drawing the reader down to murky depths. These are tales of pain in a minor key, often open-ended and concerned with a menacing psychic undertow of loneliness, alienation, fear, impotence, and the emptiness that yawns between the hours. Lacking a sense of identity or presence in their own lives, yearning for intimacy or a sense of meaning, Rimbereid's characters struggle with a profound need to be visible and to gain control of their own bodies, emotions and actions. In this they share many of the fundamental concerns of 'modernity' itself.

As a genre, the short story is generally oriented around an individual – compact at plot level and relatively uniform in perspective and stylistic tone. Rimbereid's only novel to date, *Som solen vokser* (As the sun grows, 1996), covers a wider range of material and is more complex in its themes. Over a number of weeks in the summer of 1994, the tale follows an unemployed, married, male narrator living in an unnamed Norwegian town reminiscent of Stavanger. Most of his energy is spent collecting documentation about the Holocaust – the most commented on and impenetrable genocide in the history of mankind. But the information is insufficient. The massacre of the Jews is an equation that has no solution. Finally, the protagonist realises that his primary task in life is not to immerse himself in the monstrous and the incomprehensible but to experience more fully his own life, and to be there for his pregnant wife.

Most of the short stories in Rimbereid's second collection, *Kommende år* (Years to come, 1998), take the form of intense inner monologues with a compact, realistic feel. The main character is often a middle-aged man who adopts the passive role of an observer of the world around him. In these tales the fullness of mood and the rhythmic, poetic language are often more striking than external drama; the focus on the unspoken, indistinct foreboding is more evocative than writing about the brightly obvious or entertaining. As a short story writer, Rimbereid is still operating within a dark, modernist narrative tradition, where fear and alienation are present, the ability to live with others falters, happiness is elsewhere, and death threatens.

The final short story, 'Opp ned' (Up down), is the best example of the ambiguity and pulsating pathos that colour Rimbereid's language in these disquieting short pieces. Its rhythmic touch is so striking that it comes as no surprise that the author has also made a debut as a poet, with *Seine topografier* (Late topographies, 2000). The title, the choice of motifs and the use of the Stavanger dialect emphasise that this is topographical free verse anchored in a particular geographical environment. Everyone develops within tangible landscapes – whether urban or rural. The poet brings together notions of the past, present and future with collective experiences, local mythology, objects of individual fascination and causes of pain. All this is evoked through the sensory and the experienced: Stavanger then and now, a trip to Berlin, a dead sister, a hurricane in Denmark, Norwegian wildlife, a meeting with relations.

In *Trådreiser* (Following the threads, 2001) the poet travels through time and specific geographical locations. We find ourselves in Rogaland; on Santorini; in Portugal, Glasgow, Rome and St Petersburg. Events occur in the recent past or the world of childhood, with the poet's sensual impressions and elaborate ideas couched in the Stavanger dialect. Traditionally this language has been used in comic sketches and songs, but Rimbereid gives it a new literary prestige.

The title of the prize-winning collection of poems *Solaris korrigert* (Solaris corrected, 2004) alludes to Stanislaw Lem's science-fiction novel *Solaris* and Andrei Tarkovsky's film adaptation of it. In the long, difficult opening poem, we find ourselves in the

year 2480. Stavanger has merged with the neighbouring town of
Sandnes and is now called 'SIDDY Stavgersand'. National bound-
aries have changed, high-speed trains travel to London via empty oil
wells and the wrecks of platforms in a tunnel under the North Sea.
The hybrid language Rimbereid employs to depict this dystopia is a
mixture of Norwegian, neo-Norwegian, Stavanger dialect, Old
Norse, Danish, English and German. The poet drops some Norwegian vowels such as as 'æ', 'ø' and 'å', and uses capital letters for
certain opening words. Combining this with contractions reminiscent of the language of text messaging, Rimbereid conjures a future
language that recalls George Orwell's 'newspeak', Anthony
Burgess's 'nasdat' and James Joyce's 'Finnegans Wake'. This
demanding, critical poem uncovers the future consequences of
failure to change our current Western lifestyle.
     Rimbereid's latest book is a collection of essays, *Hvorfor ensomt
leve?* (Why live in solitude?, 2006).

TORILD WARDENÆR
A prose poem is often defined as a non-metrical text with full lines,
divided into paragraphs rather than verses. The modern prose poem
can be dated back to Charles Baudelaire's 'Petits poèmes en prose',
published posthumously in 1869. In a Norwegian context, however,
Sigbjørn Obstfelder is often referred to as a precursor, having
written a distinctive prose poem in the 1890s. Torild Wardenær,
born in Stavanger in 1951, operates within the same tradition.
     She made her debut in 1994 with a prize-winning collection of
poems, *I pionértiden* (In the pioneer age), in which she demonstrates
consummate mastery not only of the descriptive prose poem and the
imagist short poem, but also of more pathos-filled texts that take
a metaphysical angle. Effortlessly, often with a wry little smile,
she makes language sound mysterious, roving through everyday
life, nature, geography, history, philosophy, imagination and
the dream. Wardenær is often seized with the Metaphysical poets'

desire to employ vocabulary from different disciplines – physics, astronomy, biology, physiology – with highly surprising insights as a result.

The title *null komma to lux* (nought point two lux, 1995) refers to the light intensity of a full moon: Wardenær, it seems, remains reluctant to switch on the floodlights and let all her secrets be revealed. Her aim in this collection is poetry that appears clear and bright but has dark corners; poems that offer resistance and rouse curiosity, following René Char's advice that 'the poet must leave traces of his passage, not proof'. Even more clearly than earlier works, this collection establishes Wardenær as an eruptive, painterly poet with an unconventional viewpoint.

The title of Wardenær's next collection, *Houdini til minne* (In memory of Houdini, 1997) alludes to the legendary American escapologist and illusionist. The uniting theme of the forty poems is the feeling of being bound – by the body, by language, in the straitjacket between birth and death – and the will to escape from what holds one back. Everyday episodes broaden out into universal, staggering questions; different spheres of life merge into each other.

After this came *Døgndrift* (The drift of days, 1998), the allusive title pointing towards the core of Wardenær's writing in terms of its themes and motifs. The first section has connotations of cyclic time – the hours roll by, the days pass, the seasons change. The concept of 'drift' is mainly connected to the body and desire; to something dynamic, fluid, unstable.

The ambiguous, portentous title *Titanporten* (The Titan gate, 2001) refers to Greek mythology, in which the Titans are demi-gods who combat Zeus for world supremacy. 'Titan' is also the name of one of Saturn's moons; and evokes the light, almost unbreakable, metal titanium. A 'gate(way)' can be open or shut; it can represent a barrier or lead one into new spaces, new landscapes, new spheres. Most of the 56 pieces in this collection are in the form of prose poems, with long, image-packed sentences that challenge normal language, forcing to reader to think anew. A lovelorn individual once more commutes between earth, sky, body and soul; between everyday, sensual observations, metaphysical insight and visionary conceptions, incorporating contrasting emotions, surrealist dream sequences and a recurring fascination with numbers and highly diverse disciplines. Taken as a whole, the poetry in this collection is boldly demanding, full of different viewpoints and not unexpectedly making open references to other artists; 'time' is the thematic focal point. Pathos merges with sober statement; gravity with self-deprecation and sardonic humour. The tone fluctuates constantly, never remaining at a fixed, predictable pitch.

Paradiseffekten (The Paradise effect, 2004) emphasises again Wardenær's robust writing style. She retains the prose poem and the single voice, conveying an avalanche of experiences, fantasies and thoughts. As in much of her work, she employs a vocabulary that at times is linked to the sensory, at times to more intellectual deliberations, but in which the conflict between the subdued and the exuberant is ever-present, and the awareness of death is a corrective to hallelujah-tinged vitalism. The title, as always, has been chosen with care. In the idea of 'paradise' lie religious connotations, announcing the poet's metaphysical concerns and the magical–utopian experiences or conceptions that are embedded in many of the poems. In contrast, an 'effect' refers to a more scientific cast of mind and to the rationality she alternately relies on and dismisses.

Paradiseffekten comprises a variety of rhythmic and close-knit texts, including an anti-war poem and reflections on the mysterious world of figures and complex images that accompany man during his sojourn on earth. The poems travel up and down like a lift between various levels of meaning, without coming to rest in an individual line or formulation. Wardenær works like Pablo Neruda in *Canto General*, piling up words, building and embroidering, attaining a massive block-like effect via a powerful, unorthodox discharge of the imagination.

The title of Wardenær's most recent 2007 collection, *psi*, refers to the penultimate letter of the Greek alphabet and is also a symbol used in mathematics and logic; more specifically, it is the symbol of the quantum physicist Schrödinger's wave equation. Via a bundle of numbered prose poems – all with the same initial word, 'Arvestykke' (something inherited), in the title – the collection builds on Wardenær's ambitious project, switching between the languages of science, mathematics and metaphysics to achieve new insights. Unsurprisingly, it deals with ideas associated with both material and aesthetic inheritance.

Torild Wardenær has also translated work by the American poet James Tate and has written plays for various Norwegian theatres.

A WHITE WOODEN CITY
ON THE NORTH SEA
Kjartan Fløgstad

In the centres of capital cities the world over, heroic monarchs, princes of peace and national bards decorate streets and squares in bronze statuary. So, too, in Norway. But the monuments in her provincial cities are more influenced by the animal kingdom than the human one. A prolific bronze fauna of roe deer and fallow deer, elk, gazelles, pigs, sheep and goats, as well as ducks with bronze ducklings in tow, turn culture into inanimate scenery as they drink from fountains and graze in the manicured forest that surrounds small Norwegian towns.

Since 2003 the centre of Stavanger has been dominated by Antony Gormley's grandly conceived and rigorously executed sculpture and installation 'Broken Column'. Naked male figures in iron pop up in the most unexpected corners of the city scene. They break the surface of the harbour waters, stick up from the pavement, emerge through the cobblestones in the square, carve their way through the floorboards of private dwellings, tower up out of the lawn in the park and from the concrete of the multi-storey car park.

Together, these 23 iron figures form a disjointed pillar more than 40 metres in length, rising from sea-level in the harbour to the exhibition hall of the local arts museum. There, the last statue in the series stands along with the rest of us staring fixedly at an empty display wall. When viewed like this, the foundation of the imaginary pillar is firmly fixed in the maritime origins of the city, while the top pushes its head into the virtual city of today.

But Gormley's powerful, stylised iron men don't have the city to themselves. Dotted about Stavanger's city centre, high granite plinths exhibit energetic merchants in bronze. They have been cast life-size at least, and are far from naked. Quite the opposite; they are well dressed, correctly decked out in the international uniform of generals seeking to conquer new market sectors. In hats and tailor-made camelhair coats with fur collars modelled in bronze, metallic briefcases, well-pressed bronze trousers, shiny bronze shoes etc., they immortalise the ideal of the mercantile class that fashioned Stavanger's trade and aesthetic conduct. As the true-born progeny of Pietism, and of the local Bergesen dynasty, they are the counterparts of Quaker capitalism (Cadbury et al.) on the opposite side of the North Sea. Instead of Bambi sculptures in the park, Stavanger displays religious capitalists in its cityscape. There they stand as representatives of the original Haugian, or work ethic-based, capital accumulation. From these beginnings the company went on to become the world's largest tanker line, sold recently to Hong Kong and Singapore, while the beneficiaries have engaged in feats of financial acrobatics with the other currency boys on the Stock Exchange. In Stavanger city centre, the huge leap from Pietistic propriety and frugality to global capitalism is embodied in naturalistic sculpture and set on lofty pedestals of stone.

Gormley's naked iron men begin by emerging from the sea out by Solastranda, just west of the city. After that, they continue in the steps of the religious entrepreneurs up on the Dark Continent. There, their silent presence is a vivid reminder that the contemporary age has arrived in the city, in art as in other things. After 1970 Stavanger's new wealth no longer came from the fish in the ocean or the fleets that sailed it, but from submarine and subconscious layers beneath the sea bed on the continental shelf. Stavanger's spaces are, reasonably enough, no longer given over to Bambis and other animal sculptures, but to Antony Gormley's naked iron figures and well-dressed businessmen in bronze. Protestant ethics, and aesthetic protest. Together they cross the threshold into the modern world.

*

As a coastal town, Stavanger grew from the sea and from the riches of the sea. Before it became the Norwegian oil capital, Stavanger was the sardine city, a name which is distinctly disingenuous as the catches that created this wealth were not of sardines, but brisling. The inhabitants of Stavanger were referred to colloquially as *siddis*, possibly a corruption of the English 'citizen'. Locally, the sardine tins bore the name Iddisar. That was when *siddis* really rhymed with *iddis*. The city lived on the silver of the sea. The sardine labels, often designed by leading artists, are both collectors' items and the city's foremost populist emblem. During the second half of the twentieth century the herring and brisling disappeared and with them the canning industry. The city was in decline. Unkind voices maintained that Stavanger had become the port for Sandnes, that industrious little town further up Gannsfjord. This was like calling Liverpool the port for Bradford or Leeds.

Stavanger and its hinterland was, and perhaps still is, the blackest part of the Norwegian Bible Belt. The county of Rogaland and the area around the city are known as the Dark Continent. In the sweat of his face the Rogalander has eaten his bread and put his trust in the Lord. And He has answered silent prayers and fulfilled great expectations: after the first promising finds towards the end of the 1960s it became clear that the continental shelf off the Dark Continent was brimming with oil and gas.

Because of the discovery of oil, the Sea's Silver was replaced by about 1970 with Black Gold. Three decades later and the Dark Continent is flowing with milk and honey. At the same time, the city has benefited from a different kind of historical fortune. During the worst rampages of modernisation in the 1960s, Stavanger was too poor to flatten its old building stock and build a new city centre. The result is something similar to Görlitz or Prague or Weimar and other historic towns which have survived because pragmatic socialism didn't construct bank palaces or insurance skyscrapers. In other words, Stavanger also possesses a picturesque old town of white wooden buildings which no one today would dream of destroying.

We could feel it, this new wealth. The flagstaffs in Nord-Jæren grew higher and higher. People became more confident about themselves. Gradually, a broader dialect began to fall from the mouths of lay and learned alike. The refined Stavanger vowels of the mercantile elite became collectable rarities; no one could try to mimic metropolitan Norwegian any more.

My first encounter with modernisation in the public space occurred in the early 1980s. I had been visiting my parents in the small industrial town of Sauda far up Boknafjord. The express boats from Sauda to Stavanger often didn't connect well with the onward flight to Oslo. Formerly, Stavanger had one hotel, with a licence to sell alcohol in one restaurant, and one prostitute, who always sat in that one restaurant in that one hotel. Things had changed by this time, but there still wasn't a lot of life on display as I trudged the streets of the city centre. Just then I saw light streaming from the door of a whitewashed timber house, up near the Valbergtårn watchtower. I turned up the steep street, opened the door and went in. The place was packed. On the far side of the room, across the bar, sat four exceptionally pretty young women who made up a string quartet and were performing difficult pieces from the classical chamber music repertoire. As far as I could judge, they did so extremely competently, playing to a very attentive audience who listened with bated breath. Like the Pietists of old, they too were dressed in black, but that was it, that was the sole point of similarity.

Right then and there I knew that the city of my childhood had changed and turned into something else.

*

In my childhood the trip from Sauda to Stavanger took five hours by coastal steamer. Industrial Sauda, with its factories and working class and socialism, was an anomaly in the religious agricultural district of the Dark Continent. The large American concern, Union Carbide Corporation, had built a manganese smeltworks at Sauda which used electrical power from the Scandinavian Rain Coast to smelt manganese from the African Gold Coast into metal for the steel mills of the Ruhr and the English Midlands. Union Carbide had its headquarters in Manhattan; its dummy company, Electric Furnace Products Company Ltd, in a postbox in Toronto, and its accounts department at Craigmore, Bermuda. Gold Coast minerals, Rain Coast electricity and Treasure Island tax, in other words. Chemicals factories, like the one at Bhopal in India, were also part of Union Carbide's worldwide operations. By national standards the manganese smeltworks at Sauda was an obscure industrial enclave. At the same time it was welded to the global economy, before the term globalisation had come into use. Ships carried the half-manufactured metal across the North Sea and up the Rhine to Duisberg, and up the River Trent to Scunthorpe. But for us, too, Stavanger was the city without rival. It was there we went for city breaks, on big shopping trips, to football matches, five hours by boat with the Bible-black farming country all around us.

On our way to the children's holiday camp at Vier we also travelled via Stavanger. I always felt very much the centre of attention on this journey. The reason was that I had an aunt who worked at the Våland Steam Bakery, far up Muségata. I would take the lead. From the steamer *Fjordsol* we walked in a tight-packed cohort up from the quay, across the square with its statue of the city's great bard, past Lake Breiavatnet and the city's only hotel, found the start of Muségata next to the railway station, and went tripping up it past the Museum.

At the bakery we were taken in hand. The firm, friendly hand of Auntie Dagny led us into the back room, there to serve large quantities of Danish pastry offcuts. Sometime there would also be some of the locally produced Isi-Cola. With tummies tight as drums we retraced our steps through the town and boarded the smack *Viervåg* which took us, high-spirited and singing, on to the holiday camp: 'On *Viervåg* we're leaving now, we're leaving now. And are we happy? Yes and how, oh, yes and how!'

*

From above, from the hub of Norwegian society, and from the seat of money and power, Stavanger, including Jæren and Ryfylke, was seen, in as much as the region was seen at all, as a Pietistic strong-hold of temporal propriety and killjoy Christianity. The Dark Continent. Strangers to the area immediately had their prejudices confirmed: for many years, even after the transformation of Stavanger from meeting-house town to Norwegian oil capital, visiting journalists would report in flabbergasted amazement that the biggest neon sign in the centre of the oil metropolis displayed the message: 'JESUS LIGHT OF THE WORLD'.

But although it may seem like it, not every white wooden building in the city centre is a chapel or meeting-house. In the Stavanger area, religious belief and the Pietistic work ethic went hand in hand. Thou shalt keep the working day sacred. In the sweat of thy face shalt thou eat bread. And you did, and they did, and we did, and the result is that we've been well rewarded for our toil. Life was a matter of prayer and self-denial, and strict subservience to God and priest and sheriff. In the wider world, the author Arne Garborg (1851–1924), who hailed from Jæren outside the city, is perhaps best known for supplying the words to many of Edvard Grieg's most popular songs. In our national literature he's the one who best expresses the Pietistic legacy of the Dark Continent, and coming to terms with it.

Religious Pietism hasn't always been so strong. On the contrary. Nowhere in the country did the Lutheran Reformation fall on stonier ground than in the Diocese of Stavanger, and nowhere did it have such a morally detrimental effect. When Jørgen Erikssøn, who was called the Norwegian Luther, became Bishop of Stavanger in 1571, he pronounced that the diocese was still 'almost completely Catholic'. It took a long time for the new teaching to take root, especially in the islands and along the Ryfylke fjords. Coarseness and brutality reigned supreme. Among this thoroughly rebellious populace, lawlessness, fighting and murder were the order of the day. Being a reformed priest was lethal work. One by one the representatives of the new faith were driven out of their parishes or murdered. The new religious order took time to get going administratively, and it was even longer before the reformed faith got a foothold in popular belief. The peasants held stubbornly to the old one, and the authorities took this as a sign that the people were seditious and let sin rampage unchecked. At several Thing convocations in Ryfylke regular riots broke out, with the people shouting that as they had nothing left now, the authorities might just as well come and take the rest. The clerics for their part soon didn't dare to have anything to do with the commonality. They were wholly convinced that nowhere were people so depraved as in the infamous Diocese of Stavanger. 'O Ecclesiam miseriam . . . O domine Jesu Christe festina, curro cito, veni ad Liberandum Sponsam tuam . . .' wailed the reformer, Absalon Pederssøn. In the mountain hamlet of Røldal, on the watershed between western and eastern Norway, the last Catholic midnight mass was said in 1835. By then the Catholic faith had been outlawed for three hundred years.

*

In many ways the shores around the basin of the North Sea form a common economic and cultural region. The climate, food and way of life in Jutland, Friesland and Flanders differ little to that of Kent, Fife or Jæren. People from the coasts on all sides of the harsh North Sea have sailed the same waters, fished the same banks. Now they meet in the open sea to pump oil and gas from the same continental shelf. There are parallels in art, too. Like Turner at Margate,

41

Stavanger has its Lars Hertervig, another painter who, single-handed, broke the mould of tradition and became a modernist, long before modernism existed.

If we extend the North Sea eastwards through the Skagerak and Kattegat, we can, and should, include the Hanseatic town of Lübeck in northern Germany in the same economic and cultural ambit. Right up to our own times, before authors such as Rimbereid, Risa, Renberg, Rein, Jensen, Harstad and Wardenær, it was probably the connection with Lübeck which, if only indirectly, enhanced Stavanger's position in world literature.

Everyone knows about the novel *Buddenbrooks* by the German author, Thomas Mann. Many Scandinavians know – or knew – about the novel *Garman & Worse* by the Norwegian, Alexander Lange Kielland. Kielland was the scion of an extensive merchant family in Stavanger; Mann was from a similar background in Lübeck. Both depict the mercantile bourgeoisie of their native cities, and both depict them from the inside. Kielland published first, and there are many indications that Mann was somewhat more than strongly influenced by his precursor in realism from Stavanger.

The life of Alexander Kielland (1849–1906) was a short one, and his so-called creative frenzy even shorter. His career as an author began in earnest with *Noveletter*, published by Gyldendal in Copenhagen in 1879. Ten to fifteen years later the inspiration had dried up, Kielland ending his days as the thoroughly dissipated and drunken county governor of Molde, further up the west Norwegian Rain Coast. Today he stands on a plinth in Stavanger's largest square, both as the city's towering literary giant, and as a refined representative of the mercantile elite that vanished when Pietistic capitalism arrived.

Encouraged by his friend, the trend-setting Danish critic Georg Brandes, Kielland set to work immediately after his first book was published writing what would become his magnum opus. In his other life he was a graduate in law from the Royal Frederik University in Christiania (Oslo), had fathered a family in Stavanger, and was the proprietor of a brickyard at Hafrsfjord near the city. In the autumn of 1879, after his literary debut, he packed his notes, forsook the daily grind, and went to the Misses Hjort's boarding house near Ognastrand further south in Jæren. There he finished the manuscript of a novel, eventually called *Garman & Worse*, which has remained a classic of Norwegian literature.

Barely a year after its publication in Copenhagen, the book appeared in a German edition. Some ten years later, the brothers Heinrich and Thomas Mann are staying in Rome. Heinrich is already an established writer; his younger brother has just made his literary debut with a collection of short stories. His publisher has asked him for a novel, preferably an epic family chronicle set in his home town of Lübeck. Thomas has brought quite a little library with him on his trip to Italy. He reads the great Russians, Dostoievsky and Tolstoy. Dickens, Nietzsche, Kierkegaard and Georg Brandes also make a great impression. And then he reads the Norwegian authors Jonas Lie and Alexander L. Kielland.

In 'Kiellands mann i Munchen' (Kielland's man in Munich; *Samtiden* 1, Oslo 2006, pp. 50–68), the author Mia Berner looked at the influence of Kielland's novel on Thomas Mann's *Buddenbrooks*. Both Stavanger and Lübeck are provincial towns, both are ports, both important trading centres on the North Sea and the Baltic. Both novels are family portraits from a long-established bourgeoisie in decline and decay. Mia Berner is herself from Stavanger and from the same background that was described by Kielland more than a century ago.

Of *Garman & Worse* Mann himself says in *Über Mich Selbst* that he 'absolutely planned to imitate it' (*die ich damit nachzuahmen geradezu beabsichtigte*) before adding that 'of course it was to be different'. Mia Berner provides chapter and verse showing why it didn't turn out so very differently after all.

At the Nobel presentation ceremony in Stockholm in 1929 it was clearly stated that Thomas Mann received the prize for literature largely because of *Buddenbrooks*. Both on this and other occasions, Mann took the opportunity to thank Kielland publicly for stimulus, impetus and inspiration. He'd said much the same at Lübeck's 700th anniversary in 1926. Even so, as Berner says, 'his gratitude didn't prove great enough to prompt Mann into bothering to send Kielland a copy of his new book.' Nor is there anything to indicate that Kielland had discovered Mann's novel by any other means in the few years between the publication of *Buddenbrooks* in 1901, and Kielland's death in Bergen five years later. The influence was from Stavanger to Lübeck, not the other way round. And Kielland died in ignorance of Thomas Mann's book.

The parallels between *Garman & Worse* and *Buddenbrooks* are so great that it's not unreasonable to mutter about copyright, the 1886 Bern Convention, and perhaps even plagiarism. The similarities centre on innate, social, and especially sociological characteristics: both books deal with the decay of bourgeois culture in late nineteenth-century northern Europe. Having thoroughly combed through several identical themes, episodes and uses of language, Mia Berner concludes that the youthful, 22-year-old Thomas Mann 'falls for the temptation of raiding the Norwegian book's plot, shape and intrigue, its atmosphere and its linguistic forms of expression, its interiors, food and clothes. Thomas Mann has been called Germany's biggest book thief. That's quite a claim, considering he's a compatriot of Bertold Brecht.'

Inspiration, loan, borrowing without permission, theft? Kielland in Mann, Mann in Lübeck, Kielland as Mann's man: at all events this was the way Stavanger became world literature.

*

Economically, Stavanger and the Norwegian coast have been more definitively linked to the countries bordering the North Sea than locally, to national industry. There has been a great deal of international contact and it wasn't channelled through state institutions in the distant capital at the head of Oslofjord.

The contrast between the centre and the periphery has formed a key area of tension in Norwegian politics. The distinctive feature of Norwegian industrialisation meant that in many cases the periphery was in the vanguard of modernisation. In the early twentieth century industrialisation was based on exploiting water power to produce electrical energy. In most cases this water power was to be found near the heads of the west Norwegian fjords. As it was impossible to transmit electricity over long distances, the factories had to be constructed right next to the new power stations. In this way they were linked directly to the world economy, without being channelled through national administrative centres. This means that modern-day Norway has been built up from small, compact industrial hotspots in the provinces.

This was how one root of conflict grew. But the process of modernisation in Norway was also linked to national efforts to liberate ourselves from the vestiges of Danish colonial rule. Working for our own Norwegian literary language, which could replace Danish, was a manifestation of this struggle – as was the temperance movement and low-church Christianity. These so-called counter-cultures were particularly predominant in western Norway, especially in and around Stavanger. In addition, the twentieth century witnessed the emergence of an organised class of wage earners in the city. *1ste Mai* (First of May), once the title of the workers' newspaper in Stavanger, was the first Norwegian paper openly to defy the German occupying power, with its leader 'Norwegians not for Sale' in the autumn of 1940. This paper was also the first to make Norwegian dialect forms its editorial standard.

The south-west's geographical position, with short sea routes to Great Britain and the Continent, has brought with it strong international ties. Archaeological finds show that this part of Norway was an important region for Viking culture. Later on, the Stavanger area was the starting point for Norwegian emigration to America. By the end of the nineteenth century, emigration from the district had reached Irish proportions. In the old County of Stavanger itself the villages were wretchedly poor and over-populated. The Danish-tainted national culture in Christiania (Oslo from 1925) was alien and remote. Emigration became a central theme in local literature. The authors Alfred Hauge (1915–86) and Jon Moe (born 1921) both had day jobs on the large regional organ, *Stavanger Aftenblad*. Both made particularly important contributions to Norwegian emigration literature. Jon Moe published *Akamei* about Norwegian emigration to Hawaii in 1975 and *Suldal Wisconsin* in 2000, while Alfred Hauge enjoyed notable success in the 1960s with his novel trilogy about Cleng Peerson, who started Norwegian emigration to the USA. The contacts south-west Norway has with the USA are still strong on many levels, and have been revitalised by the oil business. North American companies are well represented in Stavanger and are closely linked to their head offices in the USA. Everyone in Rogaland still has a posse of relations in the Mid-West.

The other main regional form of internationalism is linked to the mission. It's no accident that the Norwegian Missionary College has its home in Stavanger. Missionary zeal is the expression of a strong popular commitment and of a well-organised low-church network of associations. In this, the Pietistic tradition extends far across national borders. Whereas socialism and trade union organisation has fared less well in the Stavanger area than in the rest of the country, internationalism has manifested itself in the guise of Christian missionary enthusiasm. The collections and handiwork from many a whitewashed meeting house in the town and surrounding district has raised money to send missionaries out to the darkest of heathen lands. And in countless mission societies women volunteers have occupied themselves in what was called 'knitting socks for Africa'.

But not all emigrants followed the call and applied for jobs as missionaries. In Haugesund, the neighbouring town on the north side of Boknafjord, a bronze Marilyn Monroe poses on a granite pedestal down on the quayside. When her flirtatious bronze finger was broken off and lost, frogmen dived into the deep waters of Smeasund to retrieve the lost digit and its erotic gesture. But Marilyn Monroe didn't even come from Haugesund – recent research has shown that baker Mortensen, who would have linked her to the town, was friendly with Marilyn's mother at a completely different period from when Marilyn was conceived.

But if Marilyn Monroe wasn't from Haugesund, it's a matter of documented fact that Mae West came from Stavanger! At least her ancestors originally came from Stavanger; she was actually related to the town's most famous (and infamous) preacher, Lars Oftedal, who proclaimed his lapse into sin from the door of the largest meeting house in town. If Stavanger were to raise a monument to Mae West on the south side of Boknafjord she, together with Marilyn Monroe on the north side, would form an alluring portal to this part of the country, and at the same time an eroticised prelude to adventure in the big, wide world.

*

Economic contact has come across the water, criss-crossing the North Sea, from as far as the Baltic, Lübeck, Holland and Belgium, and the English and Scottish east coasts. After the Great Fire of 1666, London was rebuilt with timber and planking from the gate saws on the fjords of the Scandinavian west coast.

A century after the Lutheran, but crown-controlled, Reformation of the mid-sixteenth century had cleansed God's houses, confiscated gold and silver, pulled down and burnt the Catholic church furniture, there came a powerful artistic impulse the opposite way across the North Sea, from the south and west.

The life story of the woodcarver Andrew Lawrenceson Smith – Anders Lauritsen Smith – is the best example of this influence. After the Black Death in the fourteenth century had laid waste great swathes of the country and dislocated most social ties, after Norwegian political independence had been undermined and finally completely lost, Lutheran iconoclasm arrived and tore down the old Catholic idols. Never had people been so destitute. Never had life been so impoverished. Never had people inhabited a world so devoid of imagery. The artists had been hounded out of the country, their work burnt, the churches left empty and bare. The people had lost their old faith, without getting a new one. Instead, they lived out their sinful desires and copulated between the pews while the priests of the Diocese of Stavanger stood and preached to deaf ears. But it was here, right here, in this desolate, rough and rebellious region, that some of the crowning works of Protestant baroque art came into existence.

The Lutheran Reformation was iconoclastic both in tendency and practice. No relics or images were to disturb the worship of God. Religion was a direct relationship between God's word in the Bible and each member of the congregation. This was the new teaching. It turned the pulpit into the most important piece of religious furniture in the church. It was from the pulpit that the priest read scripture and interpreted the day's text. Gradually, as Protestant vehemence abated, and the state church became better established, altar cloths, inscriptions and other images returned to the church interior. To create this new iconography, craftsmen and artists were needed. In a resource-starved outpost of Europe like Norway, such people had to be brought in from outside.

Stavanger Cathedral was one of two cathedrals in western Norway, a three-naved basilica in the Anglo-Norman style. To a large extent it was the bishop's seat that created the city around it. The original Romanesque cathedral dated from the twelfth century. A city fire of 1272 destroyed it, and it was rebuilt with an imposing Gothic choir.

At some point in the latter part of the 1650s, Henrik Below, the feudal lord of Stavanger, wrote to the woodcarver Anders Smith at Flensborg asking him to come to the city to make and decorate a new pulpit for the cathedral. But although Smith lived in northern Germany, he wasn't German like so many of the other artists of the Scandinavian baroque. On the contrary, he had been born Andrew Lawrenceson Smith in Scotland. An oral tradition links him to the Scottish family known as the Smiths of Braco. Presumably he grew up on the banks of the River Knaik in the Earldom of Fife on the east coast of Scotland, between the Firth of Forth and the Firth of Tay.

The annals of art history have little to say about why Andrew Smith left Scotland. We know that the small port of Pittenweem in

Fife was a junction for timber traffic across the North Sea, and that many Scots left their homeland because of religious persecution. At the end of the Thirty Years' War this Scottish craftsman probably moved around war-torn Europe as an itinerant journeyman. When he got the call summoning him to Stavanger, he was in northern Germany where the woodworking dynasty of Gudewerth had for three generations formed the artistic centre and training ground for a Protestant baroque style in the tradition of Cornelis Floris.

What is certain is that Anders Smith signed his sacred master-piece in Stavanger in 1658. Today most people regard this pulpit as one of the finest examples of baroque wood carving in the Norwegian area. The pulpit itself rests on a pedestal representing the Old Testament giant, Samson, carrying God's word on his head. The pulpit has occupied various positions in the cathedral, but has now been placed in front, and to the right of the chancel arch. Above the base of the pulpit the panels are decorated in the normal baroque manner in three tiers, with one main set of panels and three narrower, lesser ones. The pictorial work begins with the Creation and the Fall. On the stairwork as well as the main body of the pulpit, archangels and Christian virtues are ranged between the main panels which depict the shepherds in the fields, the three wise men, the circumcision and an expulsion, either from Paradise or Egypt. The bottom panel shows Justice with her sword and balance. Charity has a child on her lap, Fidelity carries a cross, while the other panels display the coats of arms of those who commissioned the work. The royal monogram on the back panel behind the preacher is surrounded by caryatids and the inscription 'Anno 1658'. A preacher who stands in the pulpit is enveloped in a veritable host of chubby, naked little angels in lively reds, blues, greens, white and gold, peeping out from behind clusters of tassels and fruit, ornaments, escutcheons, scrolls and baroque grotesques. All this is carved into the body of the pulpit in the Florissian style. Above it, and above the priest in the pulpit, high above everything, the diadem of Christus Triumphans, the vanquisher of Satan and death, almost scrapes the roof of the lofty choir.

Against such a baroque masterpiece, the contours of the artist himself are lost. After he completed the pulpit, the Scottish craftsman-exile stayed on in Stavanger and changed his name from Andrew to Anders Smith. He married in the city and became the founder of an extensive dynasty. He established himself as a professional artisan with a workshop that produced pieces of all kinds both sacred and secular. The pulpit was then still something for guilds- and tradesmen, but soon afterwards such pieces were relegated from the hands of professionals to popular craftwork. It speaks of reformed faith, but also tells a story of worldly commerce. In the seventeenth century, religion and trade bound the Scandinavian Rain Coast of western Norway firmly to other coastal areas on the North and Baltic Seas. And so the pulpit in Stavanger Cathedral forms a chapter in the tale of how an artistic impulse spreads. The pictorial sequence is in the great tradition of the Italian Renaissance, passed on to Anders Smith in the workshops of the German masters. In the villages around Stavanger the tradition still prospers, in the hands of woodcarvers as numerous as they are anonymous in the annals of art history.

*

In his book *Norsk utakt* (Norwegian off beat, 1984), the German author Hans Magnus Enzensberger depicts Norway as a mixture of museum and futuristic laboratory. The portrait is still an apposite one, especially of the Norwegian man and woman one meets in the oil capital Stavanger. The model Norwegian of today is an oil worker and a smallholder, both at the same time. The man welding on the deck of Statfjord C in the North Sea, or boring for oil and gas in the waters off Benin in West Africa, has a work pattern that allows him to spend more than half his life as a smallholder on the land, in the four weeks he has free after a fortnight on the platform. One day he's a primitive crofter on a mountain farm, next morning he's in a business suit at Sola Airport on his way to an oil congress in Houston, Texas, or to negotiations with the oil lobby in Baku. By exploiting advanced technology, he personally manufactures the time that permits the good old days on the land to continue. With agricultural subsidies paid for out of oil revenues, he uses money to buy what money can't buy. This radical anachronism that exists everywhere is personified in Norway in one and the same individual, an individual who is both a museum curator on his smallholding and a technician in the laboratory of the future on the continental shelf.

Simultaneously.

In normal speech, fantasy and realism are often regarded as opposites. But in literature fantasy and realism are the same thing. Because it requires flights of fantasy to be a strict realist, and strict realism to write fantasy.

But is this really true?

Or an out-and-out lie?

It's certainly fleeting.

It's more fleeting than smoke.

It's more fleeting than the shadow of smoke.

It's more fleeting than the shadow of smoke on running water.

It's more fleeting than the evening above the shadow of smoke on running water.

It's more fleeting than the mist in the evening above the shadow of smoke on running water.

It's more fleeting than moonlight through the mist in the evening above the shadow of smoke on running water.

That's how it is.

That's how truth reveals itself to us. It comes over the horizon and rises like a full moon, white and unseen, behind the thick cloud layer over the Norwegian Rain Coast. We can't see it. But we know it's there, and that its position can be computed poetically and pinpointed precisely by prose. We know, too, that it's always changing and shifting position.

In 1991 I published a novel called *Kniven på strupen* (The knife at the throat). It was about the social consequences of the new, oil-based wealth of Norway. The book received a friendly reception in

Norway, and in Sweden as well, when it came out there. But there was a clear difference in how the book was perceived. The Norwegian financial press thought the book was good because it depicted so carefully and meticulously the workings of Norwegian industry and finance. Across the border, the Swedish papers praised the novel because it dared so magnificently to rise above all attempts at realistic descriptions of the Norwegian economy.

Since then, perhaps the Swedish economy has begun to resemble fantasy literature, too?

To portray the Norwegian society in which Stavanger has become an economic dynamo, one has to keep the reader wondering what's in store on the next page, and the page after that, and on the last page.

And on the last page he, or she, will be wondering what has really happened.

No, not in the book, not in the novel, not in *Kniven på strupen*, not with Rimbereid, not with Renberg, not with Wardenær, not with Harstad, not with Jensen, not with Risa and not with Rein.

But to the oil industry, to Stavanger city, to Norwegian politics, to the EU, to the unions, to the North Sea, to conservation, to wealth, to pollution.

To you, dear reader.

To me writing this:

To us.

OVERVIEW
Johan Harstad

Hush a bye baby on the treetop, when the wind blows the cradle will rock, and now the child must sleep and I must go in the kitchen to continue making the list I started earlier today, after dinner, the list of all the things I need to do in the near future. There are always things to do. There's no time to lose. Somebody's got to have the overview. Somebody's got to know how we're going to get everything done, manage it all. I sit here, for hours, in the middle of the night, writing notes; it's quiet in the house, the traffic outside is muffled, almost absent. I make a note that I must get full overview of what my accident insurance covers, and hope my youngest won't wake up again tonight; she's been ill, it's getting better, but she's still infectious.

Put xmas decorations away.
Sort tax declaration papers.
Clean and oil garden tools.
Make inventory in case of fire.

Take old clothes to charity shop.
Make jam from fruit in the freezer.
Buy Stairmaster from TV-Shop.
Begin following personal fitness plan.
Repair lawnmower.

There's no time to lose. Each day has its own agenda. The wheels have to be kept turning. If I sat down now, if I stood still, perhaps it might affect the rotation of the earth?

I sit at the kitchen table and make a list of all the things that need doing in the near future, the coming days. I see the list gradually expand, of its own accord, extending, turning into a plan for the entire year, for years to come, every single day, eternity, till the day I die. There'll always be something that needs doing. There's no time to lose. And the house needs decorating.

Clean windows.
Wash the dog in salt water to prevent fleas.
Vacuum hard-to-reach corners.
Feed flowerbeds.
Calculate additional taxes.
Wash, air and store winter clothes.
Buy camping equipment in sales.
Plan family outing.
Repair roof and clear gutters.
Book car in for servicing.

I don't know what I'm preparing for. Perhaps I'm only preparing myself for preparation's sake. The wheels must be kept turning. I don't know why, but the feeling that the wheels might be stationary is uncomfortable, like a hard rap on the shoulder. I dream my actions might be of consequence. I want you to think I'm capable.

It's one o'clock, and another two hours before the youngest kids get back from school, her children, which means it's Tuesday, Pancake Day. They've got to be picked up, the school's a long walk and there's no pavement, there have been several accidents along there in the last years, according to government statistics it's the most dangerous school walk in Norway, and children cannot be allowed to die, under any circumstances, and we must continue to send letters and petitions to the local authorities to make plans to improve the school walk for the children at the infants' school. I must remember to put petrol in on the way, find my loyalty card for the petrol station, the tokens for the turbo-jet car wash, check if there's still a spare tyre and warning triangle in the boot, in case, check if the ABS breaks still work properly, in case, if there's enough anti-freeze, check the date for changing to summer tyres, send off the order for anti-corrosion agent (as shown on TV). I must remember to buy perfume-free deodorant, soap-free shampoo, sugar-free jam. Taste-free food. I need some artificial plants that won't die of confusion from the cold draught round my window and the hot air from the panel heater underneath, plants that still look good and convincing enough for the neighbours to think I have them under constant observation. I must make pancake mix.

Buy snowblower. If the time's right.
Think positive.
We are good people. All doing our best.
It's good we exist.

It's winter, Tuesday, and I am at the nursing home where dad's been living for the last four years. This is the last time I'll visit him, they say he's going to die tonight. He's been ill for a long time, he's been lying in bed for several months, and he oscillates in and out of his own world with inconsisent timing. I visit dad one last time, and I've brought some oranges with me. In two hours I need to be back in town if I'm going to catch the hardware store, I need a new set of

Allen keys and a new blade for the lawnmower, the last one broke, cracked after hitting one of the garden gnomes last summer. It'll be spring soon, I feel it in the air, it's clearer, softer, must remember to get some more varnish for the garden furniture, the weather is warming up so fast.

They say old men get smaller and smaller before they die, as if they were shrinking, wasting away, that's what they say, but it's not true. Dad grows, and if he doesn't die tonight he risks growing out of the bed, across the floor, out of the doors, if he lives long enough his body will engulf the entire nursing home, and it'll lie there somewhere beneath his belly, squashed, though still intact. He's got big hands, they say that shows a caring nature. Right now he doesn't want the oranges I've brought. I try to place one of them in his palm, but he throws it into the wall, flinging it with all his strength. The yellow orange juice runs down the wallpaper, leaving marks that will take a lot of effort to remove.

Put out saucers of beer to kill snails in garden.
Drink eight glasses of water a day.
Scrub barbecue.
Make sure dog has enough water.
Do not sit in the sun. Repair extractor fan in kitchen.
Go to start of term sales to get the kids' school kit.
Buy single-use cameras for the kids' school trip.
Remember loan instalment.
Buy new garden tools.
Have sex with wife at least three times a week, to keep love alive.
Plant a tree.

So here I sit. With dad. I open a bag of Quality Street that I've brought, empty the small, prettily wrapped chocolates into a crystal glass dish that he got after fifty years of decent, honest, hard work at the shipyard. His name is engraved on the bottom, in delicate ornate script, with his start and leaving dates, and a thank-you for his contribution, like an obituary. I try to get eye contact with dad, but it's not certain whether he's in the room at all. It's stopped snowing for a moment, and when the sunlight slips through the clouds, it lights the whole room, the left side of dad's face, the side turned towards the window. And it looks as though he's smiling, but perhaps it's just his face, it's got folds I don't remember, they must have come in the last few days. He is staring at the ceiling, straight up at the ceiling. The ceiling is white. Fluorescent tube.

I look at dad. I've been told he hasn't got long. Perhaps he'll die tonight. Probably. I've made all the preparations, was there when he signed his will in the presence of his lawyer and a witness last month, have an appointment with one of his old colleagues, a chap who's a dab hand at writing obituaries, have written out the funeral details, all that remains is to fill in the dates, I've been to the cemetery and chosen a plot, in the shade, just as he asked last year, the undertakers have reserved a coffin his size, with a lining I thought looked quite nice. A list of everybody I've got to call about his death, along with their phone numbers, hangs on my fridge, my sister has agreed to having the guests back, I've put an order in with a company who make low-fat canapés, fat is not only known to be harmful, but it can heighten the emotional responses, we cry more after a raised intake of fat. The only thing left is for him to die. The only thing left is to lose him. I've not managed to prepare myself for that, my plans haven't come that far. And I sit here in his old chair that smells sharply of aftershave, even if it's been several years since he last shaved himself, the nurses do it, it would be dangerous to let him handle the razor himself, then we might lose him before all the preparations were in place. I suspect him of using aftershave in his hair, and turn in the chair, sniff the backrest, it smells strong, I turn back and look at dad again, he's grown small now, in a few hours I shall lose him, and I am not the least prepared.

Be a good person.
Do my very best.

Stay active.
Love my children.
Try to show the world compassion.

Dad sits up in bed. He coughs, wipes his mouth, says spring is on its way, and dad is as clear as he's ever been. I pass him an orange, and he starts to peel it, a technique he perfected a million years ago, peeling it with one hand, the other resting on the duvet.

'Do you remember Stockholm?' he asks.

I don't remember Stockholm.

'No,' I say. 'When was that?'

'Summer of 1961,' says dad. 'We'd bought our first car, your mother and I, a Volkswagen, and so we drove to Stockholm. Gröna Lund. D'you remember?'

Check fire alarm.
Check fire extinguisher.
Check burglar alarms in car and hallway.
Make plans for evacuation in case of natural disaster.

'No,' I say. 'I don't remember that, dad.'

I have to go to town soon, and I'm missing him already.

Sunshine on the left side of his face.

Dad says: 'You were only four years old, so it's not surprising. But we went to Gröna Lund, the three of us, the summer your sister was born, Mariann was born in Stockholm on August twenty-sixth, but of course you know that. Mum felt poorly, we thought the baby was coming, so we drove as fast as we could, all three of us, in the new car, to the hospital. But nothing happened. We sat in that room with your mother, and you cried and were afraid she was going to die, do you remember? You thought she was going to die, you didn't understand that you were going to get a sister, did you? But it was taking so long, and your mother said that we needn't sit in there with her the whole time, the doctor had said it might take days for anything to happen, but that they wanted to keep her in, just in case. And mum said that us big, strong men should take the car down to town, with it being our holiday after all. So we went down to Gröna Lund. It was the best I could come up with there and then, and in Gröna Lund there was a puppet theatre, do you remember? No? There was a puppet theatre, and they had a show on for children, I don't remember what, *Peter and the Wolf* perhaps, though I'm not sure. We sat right on the front bench, you sat on my lap, and every time the wolf came on, you started to cry. I sat holding you, on my lap. We saw *Peter and the Wolf* and I thought that I'd like to grow old like that, sitting on a bench in Gröna Lund, you on my lap and me comforting you, I thought I'd sit on that bench and you'd sit on my lap, even if you were a grown-up you'd sit on my lap, and I'd tell you what was happening on the stage, and that nothing bad could ever happen, and somewhere in town your mother would sit waiting for us, and even though you were a grown-up you'd be small in my grasp, and I would tell you that nothing bad could happen. Or I thought I could grow old, and go to Gröna Lund every year, and that every year the place would become more important to me, every year I'd search out the puppet theatre, that would always be showing *Peter and the Wolf* and you'd always come too, both you and Mariann. And your mother would come later, and I'd even go when neither of you wanted to come with me any more, when you had your own lives. If your mother died then I'd go alone, or with the grandchildren, when I was old, when my memory failed, I would go there with my grandchild, and he or she would sit on my lap and we'd see the performance and I'd say how this was the only thing with any meaning, because it'll never disappear, everything else can be forgotten, because this is the only thing that means anything.'

Dad has lain down in his bed again, he stares up at the ceiling, eating orange segments, quietly.

'Did you ever go back, then?' I ask.

'No,' says dad. 'But we had quite a few holidays in Majorca.'

61

Stock up on canned food, water, medicines, blankets etc. in case of
   natural disaster.
Rake leaves in garden.
Build bomb shelter.
Plant tulips.
Ensure there are enough provisions for fourteen days for four
   people in the house.
Put the lawnmower in the garage.
Buy Porta-loo. Listen to radio.
Collect all receipts for tax purposes.
Send xmas presents to people going abroad.
Shake out carpets, wash floors.
Hide enough money for two week's food shopping in the steel safe
   with code lock in case the banks crash.
Make xmas shopping list.
Repair lino floor in the kitchen.
Set up budget for advent.
Buy advent calendars from the Air Ambulance, RAC, Salvation
   Army.
Buy xmas tree.
Buy xmas presents within agreed price limit.
Go over price limit to make a special surprise.
Give money to worthy cause.
Use xmas tree as firewood.
Clear decorations.
Calculate expected income for the coming year.
Seek cover.

I look at the clock. It's quarter past three, it's a Tuesday, pancake
day, and my kids, the youngest, are back from school. I've rung
Mariann, asked her to come up to the hospital this evening, so that
someone can be with him tonight, I consider how I'm not in the
least prepared for losing him, and now I've got to leave if I'm going
to get to the shop on time.

'There's nothing to be afraid of,' says dad, talking into the ceiling.
'Meaning . . .?' I say.
'Everything.'

I wish I could lift him from his bed, take him with me, send him on
his way, but I can't, I've too little time, so I just give him a kiss, walk
over and bend down to him, and say, 'You mean so much to me,
dad.' But he's back in his own world again and just stares up into the
ceiling, and I hope he'll never disappear, that he'll be sitting up next
time, in the sun, and it'll be spring soon. But I know next time I
stand in this room, it will be to pack his things away, the pictures on
the walls. I leave the chocolates.

Clean blinds.
Clean drains.
Plan next year's summer holidays.
Carry out exercises on monthly basis, re danger of radioactivity
    from meltdown.
Contact civil defence to get overview of evacuation routes, in case.
Give children attention and encourage them to act appropriately in
    every situation.

I sit in the car down to town, look at my watch, it's a quarter to, it'll
be tight getting to the shop on time. There's another shop on the
other side of town which is probably open an hour longer, but I
dismiss the idea of going there, since my other errands are nearer the
first, and it would be impractical to drive backwards and forwards,
in petrol costs if nothing else. It's begun to snow again, and dad has
started to die, I am prepared for snowfall, the shovel is in the garage,
next to the rake, but I am not prepared for the loss of dad. And I
look over the steering wheel, look out on to the road, and I realise
that I've taken the motorway after all, I'm driving in the direction
of the second shop, even though to do so is both irrational and
impractical.

Mariann calls on the mobile in the car, on the hands-free, I push the button and answer, she says she's at the nursing home, I ask her how things are, whether dad's dead, and she says he's lying in bed still and that she thinks she'll stay the night, and I say that that's good, she says yes, she thinks it is, and then I drive under a tunnel and press the off button on the mobile since the signal's gone in here and there's no point her paying for talk-time she can't use; I call her again at the exit, although strictly speaking I'm losing money for every second I talk to her, and she just talks, talks, I give her the answers I think she wants to hear, and then I've arrived, I say, 'I've got to go,' and she says, 'OK.'

Buy music to counteract winter depression.
Buy economy light bulbs for outside house.
Use caustic soda down plug-hole in shower.
Ensure ventilation.
Plan life as pensioner, get catalogues about flats in Spain.
Check risk of earthquake in the area.
Calculate living space from total property areas, if not stated in
    adverts.
Download child filters on to pc at home.

I'm on my way home, according to schedule I am fifty-six minutes late, I must go into Xerox on the way to photocopy the list of what needs doing, and I must ring the cemetery about dad's funeral, I must ring the newspaper to inform them about the times for the ceremony, perhaps it's a bit too soon to say exactly, but I know I won't get round to it tomorrow, and then I'm back on the motorway, driving back to town, and I park outside Xerox, walk in, get a copy, it costs five kroner, as expected, leave again, call the church office, but it's closed, so I call the newspaper instead and provide them with information based on the assumption that it'll be possible to arrange the funeral for next Tuesday, preferably at 13.00 hours.

In the evening I sit staring blankly at the telly, watching a British documentary about air accidents between 1981 and 2001, its main premise being that these accidents were all caused by wear and tear in the back baggage doors, and that they'd have been prevented if the Boeing factory in California had carried out more of the recommended performance tests for aluminium alloys exposed to frequent temperature and pressure changes. I watch with only half an eye, the kitchen clock on the wall over the worktop flashes three times, signalling the children have to go to bed, they obey immediately, and minutes later they're out of sight, there are still three hours before Helena gets home from work, the nightshift, and I sit, flicking from one channel to another, Discovery, Animal Planet, National Geographic Channel, Adult 01, but the first three have got programmes about nothing but crocodiles, and the porn channel is showing soft-core where it's strictly forbidden to show anything below the waist, it almost looks as if they're fighting, and the cameraman is trying to be creative, to tell us what's happening without showing it, without much success, and I go on flicking, to one of the Norwegian channels, but it's too late, the programmes are over and all that's showing are some simplistic telephone games, automatic set-ups, jackpot of some kind, only one person is bothering to stay up and play, understandably enough, he calls himself Las Vegas, he doesn't seem to be doing too well, and I decide to switch off, just sit in the sofa, and this is the first time I can remember sitting like this, without a sound in the house, not doing anything, hands lying still in my lap, I look at the clock, it's the middle of the night and soon I'll leave for work, immediately my wife gets back, she'll lie down in my bed as I get up, it'll be warm, we've arrived at this solution to economise on the bedroom temperature which has to be kept low anyway, as low as 14 degrees, perhaps, and on the table in front of me lies my overview of what needs doing, the plans that need to be set in motion, and I don't dare to pick up the pages, to check them, for fear that it'll all fall apart, that my system won't be watertight, that the checks aren't in place, and I think how my dad's dead now, and it's too late to do anything about it.

I've gone into the bathroom, I stand cleaning my teeth, trying to brush my wisdom teeth extra thoroughly, they are the weakest teeth we have, your mouth has to be half-open to reach them, the others have to be cleaned from the gums and out, one by one, followed by a dental flossing, mouth rinse, towel to wipe the saliva away that always drips from the corner of the mouth, down on to the edge of the sink. And that's when Mariann rings again, on the mobile, the new Nokia which doubles as a calendar. I go into the living room, toothbrush in my mouth, the living room is dark, and go over to the telephone which is lit up on the coffee table, and it's Mariann who says that dad's got up and he's walking. He's been sitting in the chair for a bit, together with her, with the doctors, he's regained some colour, he's talking. 'He's talked so much about you, he wants you to come up here again, could you?'

The doctor has said that he doesn't quite understand what's happened, but that it looks as though he'll come through for a while longer, it happens sometimes, quite exceptionally, of course, but still. And some of his symptoms have subsided, says Mariann, her voice is soft and I hear dad in the background, dad is laughing, I think he'll pull through, and I contemplate how my system is unravelling. I think how it'll be spring soon, and if I can manage it, if it works out, then it would have to be organised and booked soon, but if it works out for the two of us, for dad and I to go to Gröna Lund, and if he dies there in Stockholm, if he falls ill in Stockholm and dies, then at least he could die in the same hospital where Mariann was born. But I don't say this to Mariann straight off, I can mention it later, I dress, quickly, write a note for Helena, go out to the car, start it up, turn out into the road, take the motorway down to town, towards the nursing home, exit the tunnel, stop at the lights, wait for green, and think how dad is a green man, and that for him I'll have to call the paper to cancel the notice, I'll have to ring round, the obituary needs cancelling, there's so much needs doing, the funeral has to be postponed, the lights are green, I bring my foot down on the pedal, drive on, move over into the next lane, but I don't see it straight off, that I'm driving on the wrong side of the road, and I'm hit by an ambulance coming towards me, right at me, it slams into my car on the side, right near the door, at about 90 m.p.h.

COMING HOME
Johan Harstad

Let's assume everything is perfect. Let's assume that it's good we exist. Let's assume, for just one moment, that all of us are good. I'm on the night-bus going home, I live on the edge of town, I've been out, having a beer, and this is the last bus home.

But this all happens much later.

Before that, I'm sitting in a bar at a large table.

Before that, I enter the bar, see the friends I've arranged to meet, sitting at one of the large tables between the yellow partitions that divide the different seating areas.

Before that, I look at the time, I'm running late, only by ten minutes, but I know they hate waiting and that the venue will soon be full, and for each minute that passes it'll get harder for them to reserve me a seat.

Before that, I'm alone.

It might have begun like this:

I've been at home all day. I've sat on the bed, got up, walked around the room a couple of times, sat in a chair. I've gone out and looked in the mailbox, stolen the neighbour's catalogues, there's got to be something to read at breakfast. I've sat and studied twenty-one pages of ready-made curtains, at what have to be the lowest prices in town, without being able to substantiate this notion. I've listened to the radio for a bit, watched the telly a bit. I've had a bath, cut my toenails, with one foot after the other placed carefully on the edge of the toilet bowl. I've shaved, cut my face, walked round the flat with wads of cotton wool taped to my face. Turned the radio off. Sat in the chair. Read the advertisements. Considered placing a telephone order for navy-blue curtains, two lengths, with an albatross print. I've tried to figure out whether things really go around in circles, or if it's more a case of a straight line that grows steadily fainter the further it stretches from me. I used to be the best in the volleyball team. I repeat this to myself. Like a formula. You've been the best. Once. There'd be no point in always being the best. Others have to get in there, take over.

That's how it is.

It might have been at about this moment that somebody rang, that somebody invited me out, that I accepted, got dressed, went down the stairs, out into the street.

I live in a loft that's too big, when I play music, it's as though the sounds never reach the walls, but fall in a heap on the floor, midway. Perhaps that's what contributes to the gentle layer of dust, which stirs up as I walk across the floor into the kitchen. Days can pass without me talking, without me giving my jaws any exercise. The woman who used to live in these same rooms, this same bed, has moved. She liked to sleep in a cold room, we'd go to bed with woollen hats and gloves, lie close to one another under the window, wake up with frost on our foreheads. She moved out some time ago, I've lost track, given up counting, perhaps it's years. Perhaps she had good reason. But I saw her on Christmas Eve, from my window, and there's a letter from her lying on the chest of drawers, dated recently, she sends letters from the country where she lives now. Iceland. Her letters have grown longer as time has passed, my answers shorter. Since I stopped replying, it seems her letters have grown beyond proportion, one everlasting letter, as if written on a long roll of fax paper. I am writing. A dissertation, art history. My second attempt. She left at about the time of my first. I remained, trying to fill this loft alone. But it's too big. I'm not up to it. My arms are too short. When I do the washing up, the echoes of the plates reverberate back to me.

I'm writing my dissertation. I've plastered the walls with pictures I plan to return to, architecture I want to include. I have notepads filled with research, my sofa is covered with great rolls of detailed reproductions, books about the early Italian Renaissance, old leather-bound books from the library, a steady stream of reminders have started to arrive. I'm behind schedule. I've hung the reminders up next to the pictures. I've got three months left before I'm done. If I succeed. But it's heavy going. I can't seem to concentrate. It's too big in here. Not enough people. Yet I never go out. Not like before, we used to go out every night, used to get up well into the afternoon when the postman came. These days I'm already up when the paperboy parks his bike against our mailbox stand, distributing the morning papers, slamming all the lids down unnecessarily hard, all of them but mine. I sit on the floor, notes laid out in a pattern before me on the floorboards, pink pages for history notes, blue for technical information, white pages for biographies and descriptions of pictures. An exemplary system, all that remains is to apply it. But I'm incapable of starting. Incapable of setting pen to paper.

When I go to bed, well into the morning, my feet are cold, my shoulders tense, my eyes dry. If I stand on a chair under the window on the left, I can see people making their way home. Together. In spring, and summer, my view is blocked by the leaves on the trees. A knot has begun tightening, in my neck somewhere.

Long ago, there was a girl who asked me what the saddest thing I knew was. We were sitting on a jetty by the sea, drinking beer, a party I believe, there were people out in the dark, but there was very little light, invisible voices along the water's edge, and she asked; 'What is the saddest thing you can think of?' I think I said something or other about my parents, who'd separated when I was seven, and how I'd stood in the doorway, hands behind my head, when dad asked me to carry the last box out to the removal van, how the contents of the box were much too heavy, and its bottom fell out, and dad knelt down on the asphalt, gathering up his things. Mum didn't help. She was making apple cake. It could have rained, but it didn't.

But that was then. I can't recall what she said, but she told me what she thought, then got up and left. I could have slept there on the jetty, being dramatic and youthful. But I walked after her, went home, lay under the sheets.

I changed my mind later, as you do.

But that question, perhaps my answer to it now might have been: the safety brochure on board a plane; the people always drawn without features, stoic, giving an impression of total calm, ambling off the planes in these illustrations, without panic, always solitary, never together, nobody ever holding anyone else's hand, they crawl out on to the wing, put their lifejackets on, they know that all they have to do is to keep afloat, tug the cord, then everything will be fine. They know someone will come. That's the saddest thing I know. That's what I'd have said.

If anybody had asked.

If you laid all the lonely people next to each other, they would reach round the earth several times. But we never go out. We never meet, never lie at each other's side. We remain behind windows.

I've come out. I open the door, walk up the anonymous staircase that always smells of detergent like the junior school down in town, go into the bar, see that my friends are all sitting at one of the large tables in the corner of the venue, they've reserved a seat, one of them has put a jacket on a chair to show it's taken, but people are still hovering round just in case the jacket disappears and the chair becomes vacant, and so I pick up the jacket, give it to Claus, who hangs it on the back of his chair, and a sigh goes through the venue, and people continue to stand, waiting in anticipation of other vacant chairs.

I might also have answered: the saddest thing I know is the first Russian cosmonaut, the first woman to go out into space, Valentina Vladimirovna Tereshkova, she went on the 16th June 1963 in *Vostok 6*, the Russian solo mission. *Vostok 6* orbited the earth 48 times in seventy hours. Completely alone. She sat cramped, like the dog, Laika, some years earlier. Valery F. Bokovsky was floating about up there at the same time in *Vostok 5*, he'd gone up two days previously. I've no idea whether they saw each other. Whether they managed to wave, or whether they were going too fast. Valentina wasn't even a cosmonaut, she was scarcely a moderately experienced parachutist, but she volunteered, got her place and disappeared up. And came down again. Eventually she would be celebrated as a heroine of the Soviet Union, she would receive the Order of Lenin. Twice over. She would continue to work for space exploration.
    For years.

I could give so many answers. I could say: the saddest thing I can remember is all those who were alone when it really mattered.
    If somebody had asked.
    Or if I had simply said it.

I've come in the bar, picked up Claus's jacket, given it back to him, sat down beside him. They've all said *Hi, there you are, must be ages, great you could come, where have you been, have you gone underground?* and I've said, *I've gone into the loft, I've been working on my dissertation,* which isn't true, but I haven't told them that.

We sit at the table. There are seven of us. Claus, Vibeke and Simen, Mari and myself. And additionally two other girls sitting next to Mari, I don't know who they are, but they're possibly Mari's friends, she lived in Stockholm for two years, until last December, perhaps they're friends from there, visiting, they don't talk a lot, and when they say anything it's to each other, or to Mari, but so quietly I can't hear, even if I concentrate, listen. I try to talk to everyone, to talk about my dissertation, to listen to what everyone's up to, who's done what, catch up on all the news, try to feel myself again, the old me, the good old me, try to be attentive, chat, but it's not quite happening, I notice I'm out of focus, but that it's good to be here, and I can't take my eyes off one of the girls Mari's brought, the one with dark hair, I have to look at her, her hands, her face, my gaze fixed, locked.

I wish I could freeze time. I wish I could watch us from the moon, and that I always knew where we were. I wish change was impossible.

Vibeke asks me if I'll be finished with my dissertation by autumn. I snap to, turn to her and the words tumble from my mouth: 'Yes, of course, it'll be fine, I just haven't been in the mood, yet,' and then I ask her about her dissertation, and she's nearly finished, she's written over a hundred pages, psychology, going to hand it in in a few weeks, or perhaps she'll wait until the deadline, but it would be good to have it over with, and I think, yes, right, it would.

    'Let's take a look at your arms,' says Claus, leaning over towards me.

    'You what?' I say

    'Stretch your arms out,' repeats Claus.

I stretch my arms out, my arms are white. Winter. Claus inspects my skin, sceptically.

'Just a bit concerned that fungus might have started propagating on you,' he says, 'I've not seen you since Christmas. Have you been out at all?'

Everybody laughs.

'Yes,' I say. 'I've been to the shop.'

Laughter.

'That doesn't count, it's in the same building,' says Vibeke.

I say nothing.

'Don't you ever go out? Don't you miss it, just getting out a bit? Going for a ski, going to the cinema, things like that, walking?' asks the dark-haired girl, sitting next to Mari, and I look at her, it's quiet round the table, it's the first time I've been able to hear what she's saying, I watch her, her front teeth show when she talks, it sounds as though her words come from deep in her throat, and nobody's talking over her.

'Don't you miss people?'

'Yes,' I say.

We buy some beers, we sit around the table as we have for many years, hour after hour, like we used to, and I always forget what we're talking about the moment it's said. I sit there and listen. When you shut your eyes, it's like a radio, in the middle of the table, tuned halfway between two stations. I sit with my eyes shut for some time, I feel myself knotting up inside, that's how it's been for some time, I get this feeling of getting myself in a tangle, it comes and goes, but lately it's grown, it's got tighter inside and I can't loosen it, I'm a knot in the chair, eyes shut, and I'm praying nothing will change, and think how the girl sitting nearest Mari has to stay sitting there, eternally, never move, it'll take so little for it all to shatter. I open my eyes, gaze at her, the knot tightens some place, in my neck, in my back, and I'm asked a question, but I'm incapable of answering, tongue-tied.

It's snowing outside, heavily, I think how there might come a day when it never stops, but just goes on snowing, that the snow will reach the huge windows, cover them entirely, it'll be impossible to open the door down on to the street and we'll be forced to stay inside, together, we'll all have to sit in here for months, all those that are here now, and we'll have nothing but beer and Coke, a bit of wine and little packets of crisps, a dish of peanuts, and we'll have to stay here until spring, or until someone digs us out, and we'll sit in here together, like we're in a time capsule, we'll have to take turns with the few chairs we have, and give the barman breaks, and we'll have to use the toilets as bathrooms, but we'll have music, the barman will play almost nothing but Lisa Ekdahl, he'll think it'll make the spring come faster, but he'll have to sleep now and then, even he has to sleep, and then the rest of us will be able to dig the records out from the back room, we'll have to get things sorted, set up a rota, and we'll have to go on drinking, play the board games kept behind the bar, and we'll have to take care of each other. I'll be obliged to get to know the girl sitting next to Mari, the one with the weird haircut, the one who looks as though she's got poor eyesight, and maybe she'll start getting anxious, with the days passing by and being shut in, perhaps she's got a flight ticket she needs to use, she's flying to Arlanda, Stockholm, going back home, she was only meant to be here a few days, just to fetch her things, it wasn't meant to be this way, like this, and over the radio she'll hear it's nice weather in Stockholm, people are sitting outside in the Old Town, Djurgården, and she'll be sad, she's never going to escape, I'll have to soothe her, hold her, tell her that's just how things are sometimes, that there's nothing to be done (I'll have to tell her she'll probably get a refund on her ticket). I'll have to hold her, and she'll like it, she'll gaze at me and say, *It's so good you exist*, and I'll ask if she wants a beer, and she'll laugh, not loudly, but with a soft, gravelly laugh, like a motor that won't start, but she won't want any beer, she's been drinking it for months she'll say, so I'll go over to the bar, because it's my turn, and I'll put some Swedish music on, Lisa Ekdahl, perhaps, or Bob Hund, I don't know. Whatever. And little by little the snow will melt, until we wake up one morning on the table, and see the light slipping in through the top of the window. The weather will be fine in the days that follow, and the snow will start to melt, we'll hear it running, and we'll begin preparing ourselves, everybody in the bar will be caught in hectic activity, queuing for the toilets, sharing razors, the few that were left in the dispensing machine in the men's, trying to wash clothes in a bucket, and then one day they'll open the door, and the girl who's maybe from Stockholm, though it's not certain, she'll say she's got so used to living with me that I've simply got to come to Stockholm, I've got to see how she lives there, she has a flat in Söder, she works for a company in Drottninggatan, 'You could work in a bar,' she'll say. And laugh.

Claus calls my name, out loud. I realise I've been staring into the tabletop much too long, or at her, so I look round, they're all here, everybody, the venue's crowded, the snow's not covering the windows, barely the ground, the barman's playing *Who Knows* and I look at Claus, and he asks me for the third time whether I've looked at the email he sent. I haven't. I've not checked my emails for months, I haven't paid the bill, I've only had a mobile, and I say no, but he doesn't get his answer in before Mari interrupts, explaining how Claus has emailed us all with a link to this new-age dance school, and everybody laughs, because we can't imagine what possesses grown-up people to flop across sweaty vinyl floors, with flapping robes and panting breath, on that we're in total agreement. The Swedish girls laugh.

I look across the table, I look at Mari, and she looks at me, and says she should introduce me to her friends, she's forgotten, they come from Stockholm. And I stretch a hand out, say hello, but don't catch their names, just look at her, and it happens so suddenly, I feel it lodge itself in my neck, like a new knot, I crumple up, and see that she's seen me watching her, the girl with some name or other I didn't catch, and I've not felt like this since I was a kid at a class party, I was the only one wearing a suit, I thought that's what you were meant to do, that's what my parents thought you were meant to do, I wore my dad's navy-blue suit, way too big, trouser legs turned up, I looked like a little worm in a great big tent, so big I felt I could walk yards before the suit would come with me, and my tie was too tight as well, I had to stare up at the ceiling to stop myself choking, I stumbled about the floor, I was waiting, waiting for it to be late enough for the lights to be dimmed, for it to be ten o'clock, I'd heard that's what happened, the lights would be dimmed, and they'd play Percy Sledge and there'd be low lighting (like on the Danish ferries), and we'd be allowed to dance with each other. I went into the toilets, turned my trousers up more, so I wouldn't trip. We stood in the toilets and practised, Kristian and I, stood and practised dancing, and I told Kristian who I wanted to dance with, and he told me who he wanted to dance with, and we agreed, luckily, it wasn't the same girl, and at last we came out of the toilets, and the lights were dimmed. Percy sang and I knew the melody, mum had the record, but I waited, sitting in the sofa, she danced her way through the whole class several times, until finally one of the girls came over to me, I can't remember who, although it might have been the one Kristian had been dancing with, the one he ended up spending the evening with, or the next day, the one he ended up marrying twelve years later, and she said, if that's who she was, that Liv had been waiting for me to ask her to dance, that she'd only danced with the others so I'd get the courage, so I got up, crossed the floor, and tripped in my suit, it was so large, I came crashing, lay there on the floor in a heap of material, navy-blue cotton, and I couldn't find an opening, my tie was strangling me, I thought I'd die in that suit, the tears pressed behind my eyes, I panicked, and I screamed.

I know I screamed for ages, until Kristian had pulled off my jacket and I was sitting on the floor, against the wall, I was sweating, somebody loosened my tie, took it off, and I noticed Liv was gone, somebody said her mother had come, she'd had to leave, and I didn't say a word to her next Monday, that was how it was, we didn't grow up together, so much as in parallel.

The one who doesn't have dark hair, but comes from Stockholm too, talks about the Bob Hund Band, that they live near her, and that she's been to several late night parties at their house, Simen sings in Swedish, 'Everybody but me knows what's gonna to happen,' I gaze out of the window, waiting for the snow to pile up, for the windows to be covered.

Vibeke and Simen. They've been together for five years. The subjects they're studying are chosen to complement each other, they've found themselves a flat in town, put in an offer, they know how many children they want, what their names will be, they've agreed on joint finances that will make separation a suicide mission after the wedding which, as it happens, they're planning to have in spring, and to which we're all invited. They've begun to resemble each other, even physically, like girls living together who end up with synchronised periods, they've begun to share facial expressions, the tone of their voices is similar, when I phone I have to concentrate to be sure who I'm talking to.

It's the last night bus, I sit by the window, when I see myself reflected, it seems I've mellowed, at last, the contours are softer, my face milder, and the bus drives slowly, it's silent, completely silent on the bus, even though it's full. Some people are standing in the gangway, clutching the plastic straps that hang from the pole beneath the ceiling, most of them staring at the floor, or out of the window. Here and there a couple sit with their arms round each other, some are plainly nauseous. A girl sitting near the front, on the seat behind the driver, has black under her eyes, her seat faces sideways, and I can see her mascara has run down her cheeks. I'm sitting in a seat near the back, the snow's stopped outside, begun to melt, and all the street lamps are yellow, the road is wet, and it'll be light again in a few hours and the street lamps will turn themselves off, automatically, across the entire city, simultaneously, and far away through the front window, I see we're approaching the bus stop where I get off, and I start getting ready, sit up in my seat, check that my wallet's in my pocket, and I've just pressed the bell when the bus pulls into the side, breaking sharply, and an ambulance speeds past, blue lights flashing into the windows, reflecting in the plastic seats, and all the passengers follow the ambulance with their gaze. And I think how there's someone in there, lying inside that vehicle, with big hands, and that there's nothing I can do, I imagine this person gripping the stretcher hard, its steel edges, lying there and holding tight, the bus driver looks left and right, before starting up again, carefully, he turns out into the road, drives the last fifty metres to my bus stop, and brings the bus to a halt. I get up, I am the only person getting off here, and then, as the doors open and I'm about to get off, all the passengers rise, simultaneously, suddenly, the couples, the girl with the mascara, the guy who's been about to throw up all the way, the bus driver has stepped out of his cab, and there they stand, all of them in the gangway, and for a moment it's perfectly silent before, in synchronisation, as if they were rehearsed, but they're not, they sing, one single line:

You were always on my mind.

And then there's silence again. They sit back down, everybody sits back down on their seats, and the bus driver returns, shuts his little door and puts his hands on the wheel, sighs, the girl with the mascara gazes at the floor, wipes her make-up off with her jacket sleeve, the passengers stare out of the window, at the floor, at the ceiling, only not at each other, there is total silence, and I get off.

But this all happens much later.

Before that, I've been sitting in the bar, and Simen and Vibeke have asked if I'll be Simen's best man and I've said yes, Vibeke's cried a bit, not much, just a sniffle, and Claus is going to be toast-master, and has started writing jokes, of variable quality, and I've thought how this must never come to an end, it's just got to go on. I've decided to smarten up the loft.

But then before that, Mari's told me that she and Nina are going to stay here, and that they're only returning to Stockholm to pick up their things, a short trip, leaving tomorrow, and Nina from Stockholm has said a few important words to me at the bar while we waited for our beers, and I've felt it release its grip, something has finally released its grip over me, the knots have loosened and I've decided to become a gardener, I've got the hands for it, *not even the rain has such delicate hands*, a quote from some place or other. I stand there in my loft, rip down the posters, the pictures, my notes, gather up the books, the ball-point pens, sort things for recycling, carry refuse bags down into the back yard, in the middle of the night. And I stand on the chair under my window on the left, listening to the voices of people coming home from town, but unable to see them until, momentarily, they come into the light of the street lamp, and vanish into one of the doors beyond my line of sight, I hear it slam.

Before that, Nina, with dark hair, quite long, who comes from Stockholm, from Söder, has gazed at me over the table, and I have returned her gaze, and she has taken my hand right across the table, leaning forward while the others talked about London, and I've thought how we all have to hold out, it's simply a matter of holding out. Put on your life jacket, keep yourself afloat, so to speak. Breathe calmly. Exit the plane.

FROM THE ORHEIM COMPANY
Tore Renberg

I WAS DRUNK WHEN IT HAPPENED

Hello.

Jarle?

Are you there?

The world is alive: wet foliage, drenched lawns, topsoil floating from flower beds and gardens, stripes on house fronts, sparks under the lamp posts, flooding drains. Bergen is under water, it is the middle of the night and autumn in Norway. It is pouring down over the university, washing in over Bryggen, and the waters are rising in Allégaten. But are you there?

No. You aren't.

You have sunk into a deep, dreamless state of hibernation, and you have vanished. There is nothing inside you to suggest that you exist. Everything is terminated. It is not dark in the country where you are, but it is not light, either. It isn't warm, and it isn't cold. The surface is gut-smooth and dead. Emotions have set, everything is barren. In these sparse depths only the simplest forms of life can survive. Only tranquil, undisturbed sleep.

But Jarle?

Someone wants to get hold of you.

Hello?

Jarle?

The telephone is ringing. Are you there?

Nothing is better than the state you are in now, simply sleeping, not feeling anything at all. How, Jarle Klepp, 24 years old, did you manage to get there? The warming spirits, the heavy beer, the alcohol that has pumped you full of paralysis and invincibility. You sat in a basement flat in Danmarksplass drinking steadily, stead-fastly, for eight hours: beer, gin, tonic, red wine, whisky, spirits. You felt the warmth spread, you felt your thoughts detaching themselves from their usual places, you felt your courage rising, and everything that normally seems impossible, or embarrassing, has become simple.

But Jarle!

The telephone is ringing.

It is the middle of the night and someone wants to get hold of you.

You have to wake up, Jarle.

Are you there?

It is a pitch-black night in Nygårdshøyden, a waterlogged November and autumn. Outside the windows, the trees stand bare; along the pavements the faded leaves lie in the rain. A few hours ago you were staggering through the streets, humming songs from the 90s, happy and masterful. *Here we are now, entertain us.* A drunken student, midway through your Philosophy course at the University of Bergen. With your legs wide apart, you pissed into a flower bed outside the Sciences Building. You tottered in and out of the light from the street lamps, with the pouring rain above your head and the tarmac beneath your feet on your way home to Allégaten. You came closer to your flat, came closer to Lene who was in bed asleep, and gradually your Dutch courage began to dissipate, gradually you stopped flying. You began to sink. Feet soaking, muscles aching, joints worn, mood grim. What were you doing? Sitting there yelling, shouting to a fellow student that you wanted to hear a different song, leaning across the table and talking about the American elections in the light of deconstructionism? Staring hard, and without any embarrassment, at the erect upper body of the girl sitting next to you. Then you had to go home. You were wet, you were cold and there was only one solution: collapse and sleep. Into the street, sharpen up, walk straight to the entrance door, blink, aim with the key for the keyhole. You missed, dropped the key on the floor and the noise resounded against the walls. You tried again and again until you managed to unlock the door to the flat you and Lene rent for 4,000 kroner a month. You stumbled into a chair and paused for a second to hear if she was awake, to peep into the living room to see if she was sitting there, waiting for you, angry. No. Not a sound. You swallowed your breath, flipped off your black shoes, held out your rain-sodden coat, moved around in stockinged feet as quietly as you could. Into the kitchen. Tore off a piece of paper from the kitchen roll and wiped your forehead and glasses. Stretched for a large glass, filled it with water and drank. Then you gingerly opened the bedroom door.

Yes.

She was asleep. Wasn't she?

Then you crashed out. Disappeared into a deep noisy drunken coma, a blessing for you and hugely irritating for her, who had to listen to the heavy breathing of the stinking body, who had been tossing and turning for hours, waiting for you, just to hear you stumble across the parquet floor. A few minutes later you were flat out on your back. Your mouth open, gurgling noises coming from your throat, snoring, spread out in the bed with your legs apart and your arms untidy, like a child in the sun or a Roman Emperor.

Some seconds after you fell asleep, something happened somewhere. A cool puff of air over your cheek, like a light hand, perhaps breath from a mouth, but you didn't notice it.

Hello?

'Jarle!'

The world is alive and something has happened.

'Jarle! The telephone's ringing!'

He wakes with a start from his amphibious night. The telephone had awoken Lene a long time ago. She has wriggled up on to her elbows, the borders of her eyes red. She shakes the body heavy with alcohol and immediately he is dragged up from the depths. Bewildered, he opens his eyes wide, feels his drunken body resist, hears Lene shouting and the telephone ringing. '*Ugh?*'

He knows who he is, he remembers where he was, but he is not proud of it. There is a hammering against the walls of his skull, and Jarle has a quick look at the alarm clock: 5.30.

'Jarle, the phone's ringing.'

'*Ugh?*'

'Who the hell can be ringing at this time?'

'My God, just answer it, will you,' she says, turning her back on him.

He shuffles into the cold room and Lene mutters, 'You're still drunk.' Jarle takes a few steps to stabilise himself and opens the living-room door. His heart increases its rhythm as his emotions, which a short time ago were prevented from working, are back on the job; his teeth ice up and his temples throb; the telephone is ringing, now, and it shouldn't be.

Half-past five?

He walks over to the telephone on the writing desk by the window, under the *Wings of Desire* poster, beside the draft of a philosophy assignment and a pile of books about Hegel, Adorno and the Frankfurt school. He looks at the instrument, thinking that the ringing will stop at that moment. Someone must have dialled the wrong number. You can go and lie down again. But his pulse throbs in his ears and he thinks the thought that Jarle Klepp cannot think: his mother. Something has happened to his mother.

'Yes, this is Jarle.'

He says it in a low voice, somewhat sternly.

'Jarle, it's Mum here.'

He breathes out.

'It's the middle of the night, Mum. Is something up?'

'Jarle.'

His mother says his Christian name for the second time in moments.

'Yes?'

He clears his throat.

'Ermm, Jarle,' his mother says.

'Yes?'

'It's your father,' she says.

'What?'

'Your father.'

'Dad?'

'Your father is dead,' she says.

'Dad?'

'Yes.'

'Dad?'

'Yes.'

'Dad?'

Jarle sinks down into the chair. He grabs his philosophy assignment as a reflex action; his eyes run over the title page: 'The Light of Ambiguity – Hegel's Linguistic Imprecision as an Epistemological Gain'. He turns the assignment over and puts it face down on to the table.

'Dad? Why ?'

'I don't know. They haven't said much yet. His heart stopped.'

He hears Lene coming into the living room behind him and her voice saying: 'Jarle? Is there anything the matter?' He stares in front of him, at the drawing by Bruno Ganz from *Wings of Desire*, tries to remember the poem from the film: *als das Kind Kind war, ging es mit hängenden Armen, wollte, der Bach sei ein Fluss, der Fluss sei ein . . . Strom? Strom? Yes, Strom . . . und diese Pfütze das Meer.*

Mother's voice: 'It happened last night.'

How did it go on? *Als das Kind Kind war, wusste es nicht, dass es Kind war –*

'Jarle? Are you going to come home?'

He turns round. Looks out towards the street. It is raining as if it is never going to stop.

'Yes,' he says finally. 'I'm coming home.'

Lene comes closer.

Jarle is sober, Dad is dead and he feels her putting her arms around him. She whispers Jarle, Jarle, Jarle, just his name, but he wriggles out of her embrace.

'I'm sorry,' his mother says.

'Are you?'

'Yes. It's terribly sad.'

Sad?

Should it be sad that he's gone, should it be *sad*?

He sees Lene standing there with her arms down by her sides and only now does he realise that she is naked. She is so pale. She is too thin, he thinks. She is beginning to be skinny. There are no tits on her any more. She is so petrified of becoming fat that she only eats air, water and nothing else, and ends up becoming a frail bag of bones covered with transparent skin.

Lene comes towards him as he hears his mother repeat how sad it is. She stands in front of him, a scrawny wisp with prominent hips, stretching out her arms.

He pushes her away, looks out onto the street again.

'Yes, Mum,' he says. 'Yes. Of course. We're coming to Stavanger. Yes. Naturally. I'll call the airport now.'

Lene puts out her white arms and begins to cry. She wants to hold him, but Jarle does not react. He gets up, says, 'Bye,' to his mother and puts the phone down.

'Your poor father,' Lene whispers.

He walks past her. Jarle does not take his eyes off the window panes. The rain running down the glass, the endless stream of water pouring down from the clouds.

Lene sniffles.

'Stop it,' he says brutally.

Jarle wipes the back of his hand across his eyes and feels his fingers getting wet. His hands are shaking. There is a quiver at the corners of his mouth and his eyes become misty. He bursts into tears and hides in the space between the door and the book shelf, trying to cover his face with his arms.

The world is alive.

Radios are switched on in long-haul vehicles, small children open their eyes and babble themselves into consciousness, the power grid takes the strain, the temperature rises as the sun rounds the corner of Norway. The November morning becomes light, Bergen is on its feet, and the keenest students are up. Since Jarle remained on the floor with his face to the wall, Lene has packed for both of them. She has called a taxi, put some food inside him, tried to give him a gentle hug, but he was unable to respond. They drove to Flesland with a talkative driver and Jarle talked more to him than to Lene. The taxi driver commented on both the weather and Bill Clinton – 'well, he's better than most' – and Jarle answered with an academic smile – 'most are better than most' – while staring at the windscreen wipers dispersing the rain. Lene was annoyed by Jarle's questions about the weather and the news, his request to the driver to turn up the radio. She wished he had let her hold his hand, but he hadn't. He thought it was fine to avoid the insistent closeness, her all too skinny body, he thought it was fine to chat about nothing with a taxi driver from Northern Hordaland, who could have no idea that this student, to his own surprise, had just been crying for two hours because his father had died.

'This is hard, Jarle. I can understand that.'

They arrive at the airport, early in the morning towards the end of November and stand in front of the counter. Jarle looks down at his shoes. They are black, shiny.

He doesn't understand why it should be so hard.

What was going to happen now? Dad six feet down, Dad, like the leaves and the rain and the wind. What happens when people die? Autopsy? Perhaps not, he thinks. That is probably only when the cause of death is unclear. Funeral, at any rate. Perhaps you can get to see the dead body? Do I want to? he wonders, looking at Lene who is talking to a lady behind the counter. I think I do. But Dad has died. Funeral. My God. What if nobody comes. Shall we say anything? What shall we say at the funeral when there is nothing to be said. When the deceased isn't someone you can say 'he was a good man' about, what *do* you say?

While Lene was getting the plane tickets and gently stroking the vein on the back of his hand with her forefinger, it strikes Jarle that perhaps he is the one who will have to say something at the funeral. Jarle can feel himself becoming nervous as they sit down and wait, the early-morning types around them, people with small black cases, wearing silver-grey ties and dark suits. Is he going to have to stand in front of ten people in church and say something? And if so, what?

Lene wants to hold him again; she places her hand around his and this time he lets her do it.

He'll have to lie.

It's as simple as that. He nods quietly to himself as Lene says: 'Jarle? We have to go. It says go to gate.' He understands that he has the choice between the impossible – saying it as it is – and the lie. Saying: my father lived a good life.

'How are you? Better?' Lene asks in a low voice while they are queuing for the flight.

'I don't know what to say.'

She gives him a reassuring smile. 'You don't have to say anything.'

'I mean, at the funeral.'

'Do you have to say something then?'

'Probably have to.'

'You can say something nice, can't you? One nice action, that's all?'

He watched Lene giving the tickets to the man behind the

counter. She doesn't know Dad. So far she has only met Terje
Orheim, whom she considered to be easy-going. She could give a
better speech than me, he thinks. She could talk about Terje Orheim.
The work colleagues could give better speeches than me, he thinks.
The neighbours could give better speeches than me.

Terje Orheim?

Oh, Terje. He's dead, you say? How terrible. So young. He
wasn't even sixty, was he? Terje, yes. Never short of a snappy reply.
I can remember that. A glint in his eye, you know. Personal.

Terje Orheim?

Is he dead? Head teacher at the Technical School? No! Well, I
thought he would live to be a hundred. He was well liked, though.
Strict when he had to be.

Terje Orheim?

Yes, I heard about that. He was always so considerate. Not
simply Save The Children and the Salvation Army and surface
things like that, he was the type to see inside people. Yes. He saw
inside people.

Terje Orheim?

Do you know what I remember about him? Always gave you a
thumbs-up. He was a thumbs-up type of man. Wasn't he? You
noticed that too, didn't you?

'Can't you just say something nice about him?' Lene asks again.
'Something that gives an image of how he was?'

'My God, I was drunk when he died,' he answers.

'Jarle, don't say such things.'

'I don't know what to say.'

They go on to the early-morning flight. Lene nods courteously
to the stewardess who welcomes them on board. 'It's not your
responsibility,' she says, 'to talk about your father's life or anything
like that. It just has to be a few words in commemoration. Don't
think about it. You have to think of yourself now.'

He looks at her, and suddenly he wonders who she is. This
skinny skeleton working her way towards adult anorexia says that
he should think of himself. She stands up, reaches up on her tiptoes

in front of the small luggage lockers, and her hips almost disappear. She stretches her gaunt body, puts in her travel bag and jacket, and he thinks: who is this? Shall I think about myself?

'Lene,' he says roughly when she sits down, as if she had said something indecent. 'This is something you know nothing about. I can't think about myself without thinking about Dad.'

'No,' she says meekly, lowering her eyes.

'And you've got to eat,' Jarle says. 'You're too thin.'

The backs of the seats are put into an upright position. The aeroplane takes off. The stewardess goes through the safety procedures and Jarle follows closely as if they are going to crash during the ascent. It is only a short trip from Stavanger to Bergen. They have to break cloud cover and meet the morning sun up above. It is November and Dad is dead. All he can think is: I have no idea what to say because if I tell the truth it is too hard to hear.

He half-turns his head towards Lene. Her heavy eyelids over her eyes – that was part of what he fell in love with. These heavy eyelids over her large eyes, enormous and round, set in a lean face. Where did it all go? I don't know her, he thinks, and she has no idea who I am. To him she seems beautiful as she sits there, more beautiful than earlier that chaotic morning – more beautiful because I know less about her, because she knows less about me?

Halfway during the flight he falls asleep. It is only now that he realises he had been drinking for several hours the night before, and he nods off. For a minute maybe, maybe five. It isn't a dreamless sleep, it is a light sleep during which the brain is in high activity, and he doesn't know if he is dreaming or thinking, but what Jarle remembers is how as a child in the 80s he used to wake up in the middle of the night, at home in their terraced house to a rumpus coming from the ground floor. He was asleep in the basement, protected under posters of Depeche Mode, Duran Duran and Frankie goes to Hollywood, and it was the weekend, and he always slept lightly at weekends. He squeezed his eyes together, felt the horror shoot through his body. He heard a plate crash on the kitchen floor, a chair being knocked over, the stereo suddenly being put on at maximum volume, and Louis Armstrong singing: *Oh, what a wonderful world.*

Jarle is woken up by the stewardess asking if he wants coffee. He does. Lene puts three fingers up to her light blonde hair and tucks her fringe behind her ear. She smiles at him, and he thinks that this morning while we are flying through the clouds and the morning sun hits the window, she looks at me with greater affection in her eyes than for a long, long while. But she doesn't know me.

'Have I told you about how I used to wake up during the nights when I was small?'

'No,' she says. 'You never want to say anything about the time you were a child. I only know that they are divorced, and that . . . yes, but we don't need to talk about that now.'

'Have I told you about 1988?'

'Nope, don't think so.' Lene takes his hand. 'Shh, Jarle, ' she says. 'We don't need to talk about that now.'

'I've never told you about the trip to Hardangavidda National Park?'

She shakes her head.

'No? Or the time I had to save Dad's life?'

'No,' Lene repeats as the captain's voice on the intercom wishes the passengers a good morning, gives them the cruising altitude and says that it is a bright autumn day and the weather in Stavanger is good. 'Save his life? What do you mean, save his life?' She smiles hesitantly. 'Was that in 1988, too?'

Jarle nods.

'Oh, then perhaps you can talk about that at the funeral?'

Jarle opens the plastic milk container, pours the milk into his coffee and stirs.

The early-morning flight is almost full. Lene holds his hand, the bright autumn light shines through the window and Jarle thinks: Dad is dead.

He watches the milk whirling round in the coffee cup, it follows the pull of the teaspoon, whirls from a chalky white to beige, and he thinks that it looks like pictures he has seen of the universe: the world is alive.

Then he leans back.

Closes his eyes for a few seconds.

Right.

So he has gone.

Finally.

A gentle breath brushes across his cheek, like a light touch from a cool hand or a puff of air. A nerve twitches in his neck and he gives a start. Opens his eyes.

'Lene?'

He looks at her. She is sitting with her hands in her lap.

Did she stroke my cheek? Did she blow on me?

She looks at him. She repeats herself.

'That sounded good, the time you had to save his life. You can talk about that, can't you?'

'No,' he says. 'I can't.'

WE ARE NEVER GOING TO TALK ABOUT THIS

The thing to do is keep your mouth shut. When you know what is what, the thing to do is breathe calmly and keep your mouth shut. Because you have to tolerate a lot in this world, that is what Dad said. When Jarle grumbled about something, Dad often used to say, well, you can stand there grumbling, but it won't help.

Dad is right about that.

The thing to do is keep your mouth shut.

As Mum does. Then Dad doesn't lose his temper.

It was good that Mum came downstairs to him that night, he thought. It was good that she didn't just sit alone. When Dad knocked her flying and she banged her jaw on the coffee table and then he fell asleep in the armchair, she was right to come to him. They had to stand together and keep their mouths shut. They could support each other, he and Mum. He was big enough now, eleven years old, going on twelve.

Sara had no idea what to do with herself. She was ashamed of herself, keeping Terje's alcoholism a secret from the world, and she still didn't believe Jarle understood what was going on. They had protected him well. So that he wouldn't suffer.

Many an evening she had wanted to go downstairs to his room. Put a sleeping bag on the floor. Sleep beside him, without waking him, just to avoid sleeping next to Terje. But every time she had come to her senses, for she knew it wasn't right to do that. Jarle shouldn't be dragged into this.

But now? How long would it go on?

She should ring Ragnhild and ask for help, but she didn't dare, it was too shameful. She could talk to her mother, but that was the last thing she would do.

Sara stopped thinking and went downstairs. Jarle was sound asleep, wasn't he? She just wanted to go into the room, stand there in the dark and look at him, perhaps stroke his hair before leaving, feel that something was working.

Jarle was lying in bed with his eyes open when she came over to his bed. It was just as if he had been expecting her, she thought, and she heard him say, 'What is it, Mum? Should you be here? Do you want to sleep in my bed?'

He understood it now. Mum had never fallen down the stairs, and Dad's eyes glowed at the weekend because he stopped off at the Vinmonopol every Friday after work. He came in the door of their terraced house, said 'Hi' to Jarle and went up to his office where he hid two bottles of Smirnoff Blue behind the typewriter.

Jarle understood it now, and tidying the room didn't help.

But it still didn't get any easier. It was simpler when he thought Mum was in a grumpy mood, when he thought his father was the best in the world. Because, of course, he still was. When the weekdays came, he was still the best. It was just that Jarle was no longer frightened of the dark, but of Dad. The unpredictability of life was no longer mystical, like deep forests, fairy tales and sagas, it was hard and real, and it was all about his father. He had understood that Dad drank, that Dad wasn't good to Mum, but why was he good to Jarle then? Why did he have to drive him to football training all the time, be great with him and the other boys, if he wasn't good to Mum?

Occasionally he used to think he could say that to Dad, after he had had a lie-down after dinner and was about to watch Comedy Night on TV, for example. He used to think he could stand up in front of his father, put on his best smile and say it. Hi Dad. Can't you be as great to Mum as you are to me?

But he didn't dare.

Perhaps he could make a suggestion? Something which would help, would distract them – Mum and Dad could make something together for instance, maybe build something in the garden, a shed perhaps.

No.

It was best to keep your mouth shut.

One night Jarle dreamed there was a knock at the basement door. In the dream he was small, much smaller than usual. The knocking became more insistent and he went out into the hall, wearing socks and a jacket. He reached for the door handle and just as he opened the door to the cold, dark night he peed himself, and a man was standing there, and it wasn't Dad, but he looked like Dad, and the man said, 'You must never tell this to anyone.' Jarle peed in his bed as he was dreaming, but he answered the man, 'No, I'll never tell a living soul.'

There is a lot you have to tolerate in this world.

You have the choice. Jarle knew that. Either you are a young boy and don't understand a thing. Or you are eleven years old, going on twelve, and behave like an adult. The thing to do is keep your mouth shut.

As Mum did.

Take last weekend, when Jarle had been allowed to stay up longer than usual and watch the crime slot on TV, and Dad fell asleep on the sofa. Jarle had looked over at Mum, who just nodded and went 'Shhh.'

They were quiet, they sat in silence watching television, but Dad woke up later. He rolled over, talking loudly with the voice Jarle recognised from when he was small and lying by the deep-freeze without being able to understand anything at all. Dad cleared his throat and sat up on the sofa looking at him. His eyes shining.

'Well, well,' Dad said.

Mum's eyes wandered off, Jarle thought.

'Well, well, well, that was that.'

Mum continued to watch TV.

'So you're still up, are you, young man?' Dad said with a smile.

Mum's eyes wandered off again, Jarle thought.

'Yes.'

'Well, well, well,' Dad said again, slowly. 'My goodness, Sara,' he winked at Jarle. 'Are you here, too?'

Jarle glanced over at his mother, didn't quite know whether to smile or not, so he made an attempt at a wink, as his father had done.

'Hi, Sara. Are you there, Mummy Cunt?'

Jarle could see his mother swallow hard and almost chew her own tongue.

'Hi, Sara, are you there or am I talking to the sofa?'

Now Mum was nodding, he could see.

'You know, Jarle . . .' Dad held back. He wasn't smiling any more; he had a nasty expression on his face. Dad leaned forward, until he was looking Mum in the face: 'While I have you here, Sara, your pudendum, where did you get it sewn up – at Ragnhild's?'

Mum didn't answer. She didn't look at Dad, she didn't make any comment. Instead she looked at Jarle and asked: 'It'll soon be time to go to bed. Do you want some ice cream before you go downstairs?'

'Yes, please,' Jarle said.

They had stopped singing *Jeg vet en deilig have, der roser står i flor* – I know a lovely garden where the roses are in bloom. Jarle was not a little boy any more, but his mother always went downstairs and said 'Goodnight'. She spread his duvet over him and wished him a good night's sleep.

'But Mum?'

'Mmhmm?'

'What's a cunt?'

'Jarle, please. Go to sleep now.'

'But Mum. What is Ragnhild sewing? Is she going to visit us again soon? I like her even if Dad doesn't. Will you ring Ragnhild? Shall I ring her for you? I just don't like the things Dad does, and I don't think you're moody. I don't.'

'Jarle. Jarle.' Sara tried to catch the boy's eye; he had started to cry. She held him in her arms. 'Now and then,' she said, 'we just have to look the other way, don't we.'

He nodded.

'Sometimes,' she went on, 'people are simply not themselves. And if we don't look at them, perhaps they'll become themselves again.'

That was well put.

It is exactly what he thinks himself, but in a different way.

Tolerate. Keep your mouth shut. Look away.

So my father will become Dad again.

That is what he is waiting for. He feels grown-up now when he understands what the adults are doing. Things are not always so easy, as Dad says. He will soon be twelve and his understanding of what is going on is not so insignificant, and he has understood one thing: what has begun can soon come to an end. In spring he had mumps, then it passed. He had Grandpa right up until last year, then he died. He was in goal at first, then he was a striker. He was in love with Marianne, then it finished. The end and goodbye are never far away. So that's where he puts his trust, that one day he will wake up and see Dad has returned, Mum and Dad will talk and Dad will be good to her again. One day he won't need to drink so much any longer, Jarle is sure about that. All he has to do is stay calm, do as Dad says and bite his tongue.

Some weekends he thinks it has stopped. Like the Saturday Dad was standing in the car port washing the car, without that shiny look in his eyes, without going up and down to his office.

'Let's go for a little drive, Sara!'

The voice reached them in the utility room in the cellar where they were waiting for the tumble drier to finish so that Jarle could have his football kit. They peered though the window. Dad was standing and shaking his head.

'Eh, Sara! What about going to town? It's so long since we've done that. Isn't there anything you need? Don't you need new clothes?'

Jarle stared at the rotating drum and tried to hide a smile. He knew immediately, even before Mum realised.

'Yes, but we have to go shopping, Jarle and I, and he has to go to Kalhammeren and play football.'

'Oh, we'll have to skip that for once,' Dad said, squeezing the sponge. 'He's never missed a game. We need a bit of time together, don't we, eh? Just the three of us?'

Jarle didn't take his eyes off the drum, he just sensed what he could understand, clenched his teeth and knew, he knew: it's over now. Everything will start again.

He gently put his hand in his mother's.

'Yes, Mum, don't you? Isn't there anything you need?'

Sara shrugged her shoulders. 'Me?'

'And you, Jarle? What about the cassette you were nagging us for?'

Had he caught that correctly? Jarle wanted a cassette?

'Yes . . .'

Terje put down the bucket and shook his hands, spraying the soap into Mum's face.

'Yes. What are we waiting for?'

During the drive to town Jarle sat looking at his mother, trying to make eye contact with her, so that they could nod to each other and agree that now it was all over.

Terje grasped the steering wheel with his small hands. It was spring outside. He rolled down the window, pointed at the funfair they were setting up by Siddis Ice Arena, said they would have to go there one day and pointed at the people walking around Lake Mosvann.

'A konditori?'

The clear blue eyes sparkled, and he turned to Sara.

'Doughnuts, teacakes, almond fingers – you can remember that surely! When I met you, you couldn't walk past a cake shop without your tongue smacking against your palate.'

Jarle heard his mother laugh, the stuttering laugh leapt out, it was like small rubber balls hitting the windscreen, bouncing off the roof and continuing to bounce around the car.

'Right, so let's go to a konditori!' Terje said, slapping his hands against the steering wheel. 'Konditori, konditotri, kondatritro! But first of all something for you. What would you like?'

'But Terje, I . . .'

'Shall we drive up to your mother's? Long time since we've been to see Else.'

'No, we don't need to do that,' Sara said meekly. 'But I could do with a new coat. If you want to . . .'

'Want to? Of course I want to! Shouldn't my wife have a new coat? Jarle, shouldn't Mummy have a new coat?'

'Yes, she should!'

They parked beneath Valberg Tower, walked across the cobbled stones in Kirkegaten. The first thing Jarle caught sight of was the record shop on the corner: Fåssen.

'Oh, yes,' Terje said, patting Jarle on the head. 'We'll pop in before they close. First of all, Mummy needs a coat.'

They trawled up and down the streets until Mum found one which was not too expensive and looked really nice. Then they went to the cake shop where Jarle had cocoa and a bun while Mum had a teacake and drank coffee and Dad finally had a cigarette.

Dad winked at Jarle.

Jarle pretended not to see.

'So. Goodness, we probably won't make the record shop now. What do you say, Sara?'

She smiled. 'Noo, I don't think we will.'

Jarle swallowed the rest of the bun, slurped down the cocoa and jumped to his feet.

'Yes, we will!'

Up Kirkegaten they all went, the Orheim family, and the tough weekends are forgotten. It is over, Jarle doesn't give it another thought, because it obviously is, everyone can see that, here they are, the Orheim family, and they are no different from other families, they are just as happy as all the others, can't you see? This is my mother, see how nice she looks in her new coat. And this, this is my father! Just so that you know, Stavanger, this is my father! Into Fåssen, to the counter, queue up, hands sweating, this is Jarle's fourth cassette, a proper one, one with a cover and pictures and texts. He has three more – by Stavangerensemblet, which Uncle Steinar gave him for his tenth birthday; Blondie, which Uncle Steinar gave him for Christmas, and the Monroes, which he bought with the money he earned delivering newspapers. And now this will be the fourth, which he has wanted ever since last year. He moves forward to the counter, behind which stands a thin man with very little hair and, as clearly as he can, because he has been practising, he says:

'*Seven and the Ragged Tiger* by Duran Duran.'

The cassette is put into his hands, Dad pays, and it is his, all his. No one can take it from him, he is going to listen to it when he gets home, when he goes to bed in the evening, when he gets up in the morning, and on Monday he is going to tell Leif Tore, Thomas and Marianne that he, Jarle Orheim, has *Seven and the Ragged Tiger* by Duran Duran.

Because now it is over.

They leave the record shop, and Jarle sees Mum smile at Dad as she points to a shop across the road, and Dad shakes his head, gently, not firmly, as he says, 'Okay, okay.' They stroll down to the jeweller's where Mum wants to show Dad something, and Dad says, 'I suppose you think I am made of money now, do you, Sara?' But he doesn't say it nastily, just gently, and Mum says 'Not at all, not at all, but you should see it anyway.'

'I'll go and look at the troll,' says Jarle.

They nod, and he crosses the street, to the big wooden troll in front of Arnt Michalsen. The bent troll with the long nose and the hiking stick, which the tourists always stand in front of when they take snaps. He is taller than the troll now. He is holding a Duran Duran cassette in his hand and the troll seems old, he thinks, old and small. He feels disappointed, it is as if it doesn't work any longer. It just stands there looking at him, lifeless and small, and all he can think about is the Duran Duran cassette and how good it must be, because he has seen the single from it, *The Reflex,* on Sky at Leif Tore's house, he has recorded it off the radio, and it is dead good.

'Jarle?'

He turns round. A lady and a man are standing in front of him. They are old, he thinks, and his eyes wander. Does he know them? The lady has white, wavy hair; her cheeks and forehead are wrinkled. She squats down in front of him. Big, round eyes. She looks strange, as if on the verge of crying, then she repeats his name: 'Jarle?'

'Hello,' he says, bewildered.

'Is it you?'

The man standing directly behind her clears his throat, but he, too, is looking at Jarle. He seems stern, Jarle thinks, he has severe eyes. He has the feeling he has seen him before. He is wearing a brown suit, polished shoes, and in contrast to the woman crouching beside him and saying his name, with the watery eyes, the old man hasn't got any wrinkles, even though everyone can see that he is old.

'Is it you?'

Jarle wants to get away. He thinks it is horrible that two old people stand in front of him, asking him if it is him, he thinks the woman is spooky, spooky because she keeps staring at him, as if she owned him, as if he were hers, and the man behind her frightens him, the stern man studying him with severe eyes.

'Come on, Johanne. We have to go. That's enough. Bye bye, Jarle.'

'Stop that,' he hears the woman say. 'Let me have another look at him!'

'Don't you understand?' the man says sternly. 'This is unpleasant for all concerned. Come on. Now. Immediately. Take care, Jarle, and say hello to your mother from Gunnar and Johanne.'

Jarle stands by the wooden troll, unable to move. He feels the woman put her arms around him, and he is unable to say anything. He sees Mum and Dad coming out of the shop, he wants to call them, but what should he say? The lady is squeezing him tight, so what should he say? Then he sees his mother stop dead in her tracks on the other side of the street, he sees her shoulders jerk, and Dad – what is Dad doing? He glances in Jarle's direction, a furious glance, and Jarle senses that it is starting again. Everything that finishes starts again, only because he is standing there and cannot get away, embraced by a sniffling old lady with white hair and wrinkled cheeks. Jarle feels her chin against his shoulders, sees his father charging across the street without looking at him, the old man or the sobbing lady. Dad hurries into the multi-storey car park, and the only thing Jarle can do is close his eyes and cling tightly to the cassette he is going to play when he gets home.

He can hear his mother coming, hear her saying, 'I'm sorry, dear, I'll have to take him with me,' and he can feel the old lady's arms releasing him, her outstretched fingers fumbling for his cheeks. Now Mum is holding his hand. He is no longer eleven years old, he feels like a small boy, but he doesn't want to open his eyes; Mum in one hand, the cassette in the other, Dad in the car park and the stern man behind the old lady with the wavy hair. Then he hears the man say, 'We have always regarded you highly, Sara. You must never doubt that,' and once again he can feel the old lady's gentle fingers stroking his cheek, hear her sniffling as she says, 'Will this never end?'

Jarle opens his eyes.

'I've got a cassette,' he says.

The old lady places two fingers across her mouth and smiles.

'Duran Duran,' Jarle says.

The old lady with the wavy hair nods and blinks.

'And my grandmother is dead,' Jarle says. 'She died when I was small, that's why I can't remember her, and my grandfather did that, and he died when I was even smaller, but he deserved it because he dug his own grave, and in the end he was left on his own, and my grandmother was the one to suffer, who had never done anyone any harm, quite the opposite, she was the kindest person in the world, but now we have to go because Dad is waiting in the car park.'

Sara takes Jarle by the hand, and they walk up the street. Quickly, Jarle thinks. Now we are walking quickly and we are never going to turn round, and we are never going to talk about this.

FROM **WHITE DWARVES. BLACK HOLES**
Sigmund Jensen

85

Varanasi pulsated, as it had done for thousands of years. That, too, would die and be resurrected, I thought over lunch; I didn't believe in all that talk about the eternal city. Reduce the city to rubble, and new structures are soon erected over the old ones. Erase its memory and history, and they are resurrected in the archaeologist's watchful turns of the shovel. Wipe it out completely, like Atlantis, and what is wiped out, or a notion of it, soon produces its own myths. That is how religion, too, comes into existence; the newest religions are derivations of the old. But it doesn't have to mean there is nothing to be said for it.

Later that day I travelled to Sarnath, Buddha's birthplace, about ten kilometres north of Varanasi. I could take no more of Usha, Ganga Ma, Maya, mantra, moksha and murmuring prayers. I had to get away for a few hours, and decided to visit the famous fig tree where Siddharta Gautama, according to tradition, preached his very

. sermon to an audience of five. In the year 588 BC, Siddharta sat ₁own beneath the Tree of Enlightenment, legs crossed, because he needed to rest after six years of wandering the world – according to the guide who among the crowd of enthusiastic tour guides stuck to me like glue and won the competition to show me around for a dollar.

'Here he was rewarded with nirvana,' the guide said reverentially.

Perhaps I too could be rewarded with the gift of enlightenment, just as incidentally, I thought, as I was leaning against a tree-trunk in the vicinity of the holy fig tree.

I didn't notice him at first, the sadhu who sat some distance off.

'Sahib!' he called to me. Then he rattled off a stream of words I didn't understand.

'What's he saying?' I said.

'He wants you to come to him,' the guide said.

Even if the sadhu was an old and toothless man, he exuded a kind of authority that made it difficult to defy him.

'One day, unforeseeable to the human race, Vishnu returns as Jagannath to rule over mankind,' he said, when we had sat down.

'Is he Hindu?' I asked, turning to the guide, who confirmed it with a smile. 'What's he doing here then?'

'He's listening to the voices of history.'

Then the old man spoke at length about the fourfold way. Apparently I could wander the way of enrapture without his or any other wise man's help. To choose the way of action was as good as giving up one's self. Should I decide to go the way of knowledge, I would need the guidance of a guru, and then he, Badarayan, which was his name, was at my disposal, and would explain to me the essence of Brahman, Atman and the universe. Or I could wander the way of the yoke and, through the Hatha yoga's eight stages, achieve Samadhi, a higher consciousness.

'I'm going my own way,' I said.

'You've still probably paid a visit to all of them,' he said.

'In that case I must've left them by now,' I said.

'So you think moksha is unobtainable,' he smiled, and looked at my guide, who agreed with the sadhu by smacking his lips. I felt a strong distaste at the situation. On the one hand I wanted to get away from there, away from this cool palm grove with the holy fig tree that gave me so many uncomfortable religious associations. I hoped the guide would come to my rescue, but he was obviously much too well-mannered. On the other hand, face to face with Badarayana, who sat in the lotus position and puffed lazily on a bhang, something held me back, something that nailed me to the spot and held my attention.

'Both yoga and jnana lead to expansion of one's consciousness,' the old man said. 'But you also need the blessing of the river. I can see that's how it is. You are grieving. Tomorrow you shall bathe in the river, do puja, and the river goddess Ganga will wash away your sins, cleanse your wounds, wipe away your doubt and make you a seeing man.'

He stood up and bowed lightly to me.

'I'll leave now, sahib,' he said. 'Remember, what you need most, you have within yourself. The river will help you with the rest.'

His thin back disappeared between the palms. I looked at the guide.

'What a fool,' I mumbled.

I sent the guide away with a dollar and lay down. I concentrated on inhaling the light, the air, the colours. I looked at the fig tree again and thought about the gospel of Matthew: *By their fruits ye shall know them. Do men gather grapes of thorns or figs of thistles?*

I knew that somehow I had to get over to the other side.

86

She began the day by throwing up, usually before dawn. She rarely slept more than three or four hours a night. She spent the mornings in spasms and tears, the afternoons restlessly wandering through the streets or in Hyde Park. She didn't get better. She ate almost nothing. The scales spoke their plain language. She shrank more and more for every day. She brought up half of every meal. She lived with constant nausea and felt like retching at the least sign of stress. Her decision, or what she understood to be her decision, was not in accordance with reality. But how could it be, as long as her decision was still something indefinable and unresolved But one day she said, 'I want everything to be as before.'

I thought to myself that it never would be, not after this, but I said, 'All in good time.'

She held her head in her hands and started to cry.

'We have to go to Cornwall this summer, Gestas. You must promise me that.'

I nodded.

'We have to stay there for the whole summer,' she said. 'It's so nice there. Do you promise me that, Gestas?'

'Yes,' I said. 'I promise.'

For a long time she tried to keep up the daily routines, but as time went by it became hopeless. The absurdity of her existence confronted her everywhere, at home, in the shops, at work, in the pub, in all forms of distractions. She was weighed down by the inconceivable burden of meaninglessness. There was nothing I could do.

We parted without any song and dance, a real happy ending.

The aggression that gradually built up inside me, layer upon layer, like sediments in a valley, was of the hateful and bitter kind and obviously had to be tamed. She didn't use the moments of serenity that her suffering granted her from time to time, suddenly and without any discernible pattern, in any fruitful way, but only to pick on my looks and my behaviour. 'You must go to the hairdresser,' she could say in these lucid moments. 'That shirt doesn't suit you,' she could say. Or 'You mustn't drink so much,' although to every outsider it was as clear as day that the whisky just served as my form of Valium, Prozac or god-knows-what. From time to time I caught myself thinking that she was more attractive when she was an angst-ridden and helpless girl than when she was her usual self, that is, this grim pedant who instead of kids and a dog had found herself a man to pick on. Perhaps she thought that if she could only get me to fit the image she had of me, the pieces would fall into place in her own chaotic mind. I don't know. It was such a fundamental feature of her character, yes, such an intrinsic part of most women, in my opinion, that it was hopeless to fight against it.

Finally, I couldn't even be bothered to remind her to eat.

87

That evening I met Stanley, a villainous Reuters photographer from Manchester. Tall, dark and with an unpolished charm, he acted as a magnet to women who didn't seem to worry that he was trading in suffering. He had been to every continent and covered every conflict. As the years passed he had developed a fondness for the war-wounded, *the still-suffering*, as he called them, and preferably those with torn-off limbs. He was particularly proud of a photograph he had taken in Eritrea. It showed a soldier at the exact moment a projectile from a sniper deprived him of his life. Stanley had even managed to capture the blood that spurted out through the exit wound in the soldier's back.

'What can I say?' he said, casually sprawled across the bar counter in his worn khaki pants and a military-green vest of the sort that seemed to be reserved for photographers, ornithologists, commandos and hobby fishermen. 'A picture says more than a thousand words.'

'I prefer to put it like this,' I said, 'there are too many pictures in circulation in the world. Every photograph casts a shadow over the previous one. Too many pictures have a saturating effect.'

'You have to use strong means to make people react,' he said. 'I think that's a misunderstanding,' I said. 'On the contrary, when you use strong means, people feel a need to protect themselves.' We sat for a while at the bar and talked about the art of photography. Stanley stressed the duty to publish, he felt it was his calling to document poverty, violence and suffering. I, on the other hand, argued strongly that those kinds of motifs were now too much of a good thing, and that all he achieved was to degrade the people he photographed.

'Every time you take a picture of a mutilated soldier or a child in the gutter,' I said, 'you steal a little of the child's and the soldier's dignity.'

'Well, I'm afraid that's the kind of pictures the news desk wants,' he sighed. 'You've got to earn a crust somehow.'

I sat and listened to him with a somewhat punctured feeling that nothing led anywhere. Everything repeated itself. The most recent bullet to the neck was the previous decapitation's déjà vu. Stanley and Winterbottom were in the same business, but they imparted nothing new or fresh. Haven't the so-called news merely been repeated across the centuries? Every day the same events – rumours about war and hunger catastrophes, new war declarations – replace the old ones that no one remembers the reasons for any more, oil prices that go up and down haphazardly, fortune tellers who mutter vague predictions about vanished people and lost animals, a man's sudden rise to the strata of major players, another man's rapid fall into the pit of shame and scandal, a king abdicates, a government resigns, new kings and governments are sworn in, one junta is replaced by another, bestiality and bribery, sex and scandal, corruption and catastrophes, and continuous propaganda with no margin for negotiations. Hasn't it always been like that? These are the events we report as constant testimonies of our conditions and possibilities. The individuals who are included in them are reduced to trinkets and extras, symbols which only exist to give flesh and blood to our *concept* of the individual.

After a while Stanley leaned towards me and whispered:
'Tomorrow I'm going over to the other side.'
'No one goes ashore there,' I said.
'No one but the butchers, at least,' he said. 'Well? What do you say? Are you coming?'

The whole time I had been tempted to ask if he felt a need to justify himself, but had refrained. Now I was so thrilled by his offer that I didn't want to risk offending him. I accepted on the spot. We agreed to share the expenses. He would get a boat, I would find an interpreter. We would meet in the hotel bar at five o'clock the next afternoon.

Fired up at the thought, I emptied my drink and immediately ordered another. Reuter's latest version of Indiana Jones lit a cigarette and looked at me with drunken eyes. Then he left the bar with a woman on each arm.

I stayed at the bar and began to think about two famous photographs I had never quite managed to get out of my head. One is from an island in the Pacific Ocean during World War II, and shows a Japanese officer swinging a samurai sword above the neck of an Australian soldier. I have been told that the traditional Japanese Samurai sword is the most perfectly sharp-edged weapon ever produced. A couple of centuries ago the sword-maker used to take his sword to the scaffold, where he tried it out on the recently executed. If the sword managed to cut through three dead bodies with one blow, it was characterised as first rate. If he needed more than one blow to sever the head from the body, it was deemed useless. Accordingly, one must presume that the Australian soldier's head, with one sober blow, lay in the sand the moment after the moment of the photograph.

The other photograph is more recent by a couple of decades. It hails from the Vietnam war and shows Saigon's Chief of Police pointing his service pistol at the head of a Vietcong sympathiser. The moment after the moment of this photograph, the collaborator is shot in the head and falls dead to the ground.

Both photographs show a calculated murder, ritual violence. A world which doesn't recognise the individual's inviolable rights allows and accepts that sort of thing. More than that: we have even created entertainment out of it. It is probably just a matter of time before the mass murders committed under the auspices of the state of Texas are made into entertainment, first as a news item that titillates our basest instincts, then as its own programme that unfolds the life stories of all those involved, the condemned on death-row, the executioners, the prison priest, the judge, the victim, the victim's relatives, and includes interviews with parents, siblings, high-school girlfriends, party pals and previous work mates, with commercial breaks and countdown to the big moment, a morbid mixture of New Year's Eve on Times Square, Super Bowl and the Wembley Cup Final.

In the wonderful new world it is no longer called murder, but *collateral damage*. The individual who is murdered is made invisible by brutal abstraction. The murderers carry out double violence. The war has, in the terms of the cultural theorist Jean Baudrillard, become a television game. To wipe out the last vestiges of moral scruples in the murderer, the officially sanctified murders are presented as a fight against evil, the satanic, the destructive and the infectious. The victims are made invisible and inhumane. By pushing them away from humanism's accountable universe, that is, out of the sphere which is embraced by our human compassion and mercy, and banishing the victims from the Anglo-American unambiguous paradise, we are relieved from the moral obligations that are still held up as humanistic imperatives in Western cultures. The moral *we* abide by can be neatly suspended in conflict with *the others*. A good Arab is a dead Arab. Saddam Hussein is the Hitler of our age. The Serbs are evil, the Chinese are unpredictable, the Russians untrustworthy. The ritual killing, the systematic and organised murder, is not just a crime against humanity; it is a crime against humanness. The Japanese officer offends against his own humanness the moment he lets the sword fall against the Australian soldier's neck, just as

Saigon's Chief of Police offends against his humanness the moment his finger pulls the trigger. And Stanley, I think as I sit at the bar, what crime is he guilty of?

The rhetoric of psychology, mass media, religion, capitalism, instrumentalism and politics wants us to believe that our humanness has evolved. We constantly dress in the emperor's new clothes, and every morning we look into a fool's mirror. The point of origin for any evaluation of information, rhetoric and propaganda should therefore be Magritte's famous painting *Ceci n'est pas un pipe*. We convince ourselves that ownership rights, capital, power, consumption, science, and art, too, for that matter, are the pipe itself, when they are only the mirror in which the real pipe dimly appears: ecological destruction, impoverishment of whole continents, profiteering by nations and populations, social control, coercion, oppression and manipulation, everything under the colourless banner of globalisation and neo-liberalism, where everyone is the same, thinks the same, wants and dreams about the same, and everyone has come to terms with the new era's mechanisms as something inevitable and fated, as if it is a matter of ordinary natural forces. Dante's Inferno and Maya's veil. We move towards neo-cannibalism, as if we were part of a lively St Patrick's Day parade. *The others* we devour, and the chewy and inedible, that is, those who won't be controlled, we ridicule and oppress.

Perhaps Stanley was right that it all had to be documented, I thought, when I unlocked the door to my hotel room in the early hours of the morning. We have to recover our right to feel healthy, even if we think differently. And we have to recover our duty to think differently, even if it makes us feel sick, dirty and unwell.

88

At dusk, embers from the countless bonfires along the river-bank were still glowing. The sun sank slowly on the horizon. In the grey-brown muddy water flowed ash, refuse and flowers, scattered remnants of the hectic activity on the river-bank earlier in the day. A heavy haze hung over the holy river. The breath of the river at dusk, the city like a slumbering beast, a steady and distant noise.

I was standing on the river-bank with Stanley and the interpreter, who was a relative of the hotel receptionist. The interpreter seemed very impatient. He chain-smoked and checked his watch constantly. 'Do you know what we can expect over there? On the other side?' He shrugged. We didn't say anything for a while. From between the palm trees further along the bank came a soft, lyrical elegy. The sun shone red-hot among the white clouds above us. There was a time in my life when I would have enjoyed such a sight, but not any more. Perhaps everything becomes a habit in the end, perhaps the days become a treadmill you can't jump off before you fall off, dead. I don't know.

Soon I, too, started to lose patience, a feeling came over me of wasting time.

'Where is he?' I finally said.

'He's coming,' Stanley said, but this time in a somewhat resigned voice. Annoyed, he threw the cigarette in the sand.

'Oh well,' I said. 'That's what it's like to wait for the ferryman. Or Godot, for that matter.'

'It's not a ferry,' Stanley said.

'I know that,' I said. 'I just – '

'There!' he interrupted me. He pointed to a small boat on the river. 'There he is!'

'Charon', I mumbled.

'What are you mumbling about, Hutting?' he said. He looked at me sceptically. Or perhaps it was disapprovingly, I couldn't tell.

Behind me was the noise of the city, in front of me lay the old lady, Ganga Ma. She whimpered under the weight of centuries of exhaustion, births and deaths, burdened by the weight of liberated souls and ashes. How many stories had drowned here? How many histories did she hide in her womb? Was it actually anything but theatre, this daily ritual on the river-bank? It felt like being in the belly of a horrible fiction.

The ferryman sat at the tiller with the wind in his hair and the slow, rhythmical cough of the diesel engine in his ears. A stoic, like most of us. It's strange, I thought as I sat in the boat, how little fuss these poor people make over their poverty. They get up in the morning, do what they have to do that day, accept all limitations, walk around all barriers, eat a little, talk a little, copulate a little, and go to bed at night. And the next day everything repeats itself with frightening precision.

A strong wind was blowing on the river. It was the type of evening wind that made you shiver, even if you didn't really feel cold. The haze lay like a thick blanket of smoke over the water, and when we were half-way, the boat became enveloped by the haze and we didn't have a clear view to either bank any more. But we could still hear the drums, the ritual singing, the animals squealing in cere-monial death angst.

Suddenly the boat hit something. The ferryman stopped the engine at once. I looked at him to see if I could gauge the seriousness of the situation from his face, but he remained expressionless. Then I looked at the interpreter, who stayed equally calm, and finally at Stanley, who just shrugged indifferently and leaned over the edge to have a look.

'What do you know!' he exclaimed. 'There's a man bobbing up and down in the water!'

He got down on one knee and found his balance. I thought he was preparing himself to pull the man out of the river, but instead he grabbed his camera, put it up to his face and started to snap pictures.

'What are you doing?' I said.

He didn't answer. He just continued to take photographs, as if he too had a shutter in his chest. I picked my way carefully over to him, and leaned out over the river. I saw an old man in the water, half-naked and with closed eyes. For every little swell rocking the boat, his head hit the hull.

'Is he dead?' I whispered.

'No, he's not dead,' Stanley said. 'He smiled at me just now.'

'He smiled?'

'I'll be damned if he didn't smile. Beats me.'

Stanley lowered the camera and looked seriously at me. After a few seconds I began to understand from the way he looked at me that he thought I was an idiot. He said:

'Don't you understand anything, Hutting? He smiled.'

No more than a few seconds could have passed, but it felt like an eternity. I looked at Stanley, saw how he lifted the camera again, turned it around, adjusted the lens, took continuous pictures, all the while with a strangely satisfied and engrossed expression, and I thought about him that he had to be totally mad, morally sterile, ethically impotent, and oddly enough it was as if this aroused some sort of anger in me.

'I'll have to pull him on board myself then,' I sniffed, and leaned out to grab the old man. But I was held back by an agitated and incomprehensible outburst by the ferryman.

'He says leave him alone,' the interpreter said.

'Is he out of his mind?' I said.

'Listen to the captain, Hutting,' Stanley said. 'He knows what he's talking about.'

The ferryman mumbled something, the interpreter translated: 'This is India.'

'Yes, I'm well aware of the fact that this is India!' I shouted. 'What is it with you Indians? Why do you always have to tell me that? As if I don't know where I am?'

'We deal with things a little differently here,' the interpreter said just as calmly.

'There, hear that, Hutting?' Stanley smiled behind the camera lens.

'But he's dying!' I said unhappily. 'If we don't help him, he'll die.'

'You don't understand,' the interpreter said.

'So what are you really saying?' I said. 'That it's a suicide candidate who's lying there knocking his head against the hull?'

The interpreter explained that this was a sadhu, an old, wise man who was probably tired of waiting for death. When death had failed to find him, he had decided to go and find death.

'How can you be so sure about that?' I said. 'Has someone asked him? When? Charon?'

'Charon?' the interpreter said, bewildered.

'Who are you calling Charon?' Stanley asked.

'The ferryman,' I said.

'The ferryman's name isn't Charon,' Stanley said. 'Besides, he's not a ferryman. I think you're going nuts.'

I pointed to the ferryman, and then I pointed to the old man in the water.

'Ask him!' I insisted.

The ferryman looked severely at me. I could see that he found me a nuisance; it was as if he regretted he had even accepted this job. He lit a bhang, took a couple of deep puffs and came forward.

'What in – ' I said.

'Sshh!' the interpreter whispered.

The ferryman bent over the old man in the river and blew one cloud of smoke after the other in his face. The sadhu started to cough. Finally he opened his eyes and looked at the ferryman. He mumbled something.

'What's he saying?' I asked the interpreter.

'He's stuck,' the interpreter said, without looking at me.

'How can he be stuck?' Stanley asked.

'There's nothing to get stuck in?' I said.

Suddenly the ferryman pulled out a knife. He looked at us with sharp eyes, and I stepped back instinctively. But then he gave the knife to the old man, who ducked under the surface. Stanley stopped taking pictures.

'What's happening?' he said, confused.

'Usually the sadhus tie a sinker to their legs,' the interpreter explained. 'Jars filled with sand, rocks, something that can pull them under. Obviously it wasn't a great success for our sadhu.'

A moment afterwards the sadhu surfaced again. He handed the knife to the ferryman, smiled and mumbled something incomprehensible. Then he kicked out to get away from the boat, floated out to the side and was immediately swept downstream by the current.

'What did he say?' I asked.

The ferryman sat down. Stanley picked up his camera again and took pictures of the sadhu's head drifting down the river at a fast pace. His head became smaller and smaller, soon it wouldn't be much bigger than a full stop, I thought. The ferryman started the engine. He looked a little peeved.

'What did he say?' I repeated.

'Thank you,' the interpreter said. 'He said thank you.'

'What did I tell you, Hutting?' Stanley said. 'He smiled, didn't he?'

I didn't understand them. I thought they took it much too lightly. The ferryman pushed the ailing diesel engine to the limit to make up for the half kilometre we had lost by sending the sadhu to his death. Stanley took photos. He saw the world through his lens, the eye of the camera was also Stanley's eye. Yes, perhaps this moment of life and death wasn't even quite real to him before it was developed in the darkroom. He was the archetypal new human being. He had taken the consequences of what we have all become. The flood of photographs turns us into wretched paralysed peeping toms.

It was dark when we finally reached our destination. The situation looked pretty bleak when the ferryman obstinately refused to go alongside the jetty. He insisted that we had to swim the last few metres.

'Swim?' Stanley said indignantly. 'Is this supposed to be a joke? I've got a whole bagful of camera equipment.'

'He's afraid of dying,' the interpreter explained.

'Dying?' Stanley fumed. 'No one here's going to die!'

'And what if he should die?' I said. 'What then?'

'Then he'll be reborn as a monkey for all eternity,' the interpreter said.

Well, that threw a different light on it. What is a Pentax against being a monkey for all eternity? I could fully understand that the ferryman refused to put to shore on that basis.

'And what about you?' I said to the interpreter. 'Aren't you afraid to die?'

'Superstition,' he smiled. 'I'm an atheist.'

But as the Earl of Kakinada once claimed, the problem doesn't exist which either the sword or the banknote cannot solve. With the help of the interpreter's persuasiveness and our banknotes, we finally managed to induce the ferryman to take the boat close enough to the riverbank for us to wade ashore. Thus Stanley avoided destroying his expensive camera equipment, I didn't have to worry that a half-rotten sadhu should pop up in my wake, and the ferryman could feel safe that he wasn't tempting fate. He let us off the boat a couple of hundred metres up the river. That way we steered clear of the blood and the entrails that the butchers had discarded in the course of the day. But we still had to put up with the thought of excrement from 400 million Indians.

Two parrots sat on each side of the palm portal and guarded the entrance. Just inside was a rubbish heap. On top of it sat a young man rocking mindlessly from side to side. He was known as Boy, we learnt later, and he sat and rocked incessantly, covered by infected sores from top to toe; sores he scraped with a pottery shard, mumbling the same sentence over and over.

'What's he saying?' I asked.

'I'm awaiting goodness. Evil came,' the interpreter said.

When we came to the slaughter square, the butchers were on a break. They sat around the bonfire, drank orange juice, ate bread and talked in low voices. A few smoked pot and stayed in the background, but apart from that the mood was congenial, as if these people, too, had understood that the only thing that could bring them comfort in all the misery was recreation. A young woman walked among them, her back straight, as if the thought of walking yet another few metres on this lamentable road didn't faze her whatsoever. She was reserved, but still had a strong presence. It was obvious that she enjoyed the men's respect, and the whole scene appealed to my most primitive needs. The ten or twelve animals waiting to be slaughtered tonight, mostly wild boars, were calm as well, as if they enjoyed their last hours without a thought of eternity. The haze had begun to lift, and we could see the lights from Varanasi. Spread around the square were animal carcasses and bloody tools glittering sharply in the glow of the flames. Hens' feet were piled up in the grass, the stink of blood and meat was suffocating. A distance off, in the mud and the slime, were the unwanted remnants, bits and pieces flung aside, and next to the furnace lay animal skins and knuckles in a pool of dried blood. Leaning against a tree was the drum I had heard so often. The butchers sat around the bonfire. They dipped their naan bread in small bowls of chicken soup. To them, we must have appeared as either fearless or incredibly stupid, but they didn't ask questions as long as we paid them to take pictures.

After about half an hour they went back to work. The woman tidied up after them. In her every movement I recognised this enigmatic power or pride that I have always found so admirable, and I thought, it is this feminine strength that will finally save us when the last remnant of masculine vigour eventually lapses into the recriminations, melancholy and random brutality which are the natural consequence. Then she left. She farewelled us with a (soft? tolerant? motherly?) smile, turned slowly away, followed the riverbank for a while and disappeared between the palm trees further up, before her shadow finally became one with the darkness.

I was wrenched from this dream image by a terrible shriek. A boar screamed in deadly fear. One of the butchers had got astride the beast and had forced it to the ground. Now he was on his knees in the gravel with the boar between his legs. With his left hand he held the boar's head in a firm grip, with the right he lifted the knife. Stanley photographed the whole thing. For an absurd moment, just before the butcher drove the knife into the animal's neck, he tilted his head and smiled lopsidedly to the camera. He held the pose. The boar screamed. Stanley took pictures. And all the time the butcher sat there with his knife in the air, ready for the blow, while he spoke to the animal in a soft and calm voice. Strangely enough it seemed to help, or perhaps the boar was exhausted by the whole situation and its own futile screams, what do I know, but finally it calmed down, stopped kicking and squirming, gave up any effort to tear itself loose from the butcher's practised grip, and stopped screaming. And then, just as the animal somehow gave itself up, or accepted its fate, just as the animal no longer offered resistance or made a sound, but just lay there, subdued, between the butcher's legs, it was given the death blow. In one fast movement, the butcher drove the knife into the animal's neck, and almost before I could blink from this paralysing sight, he broke the animal's neck with a sudden twist, at the same time as he cut its throat with a quick, surgically precise cut. He stood up and smiled. Two of his assistants took care of the animal, bled it, pulled out the entrails, flayed it and severed the parts of the animal that could be used and threw the useless ones in the river.

The butcher said something and held the bloody knife up in front of me. Stanley took pictures.

'He asks if you want to try,' the interpreter said.

I looked at the butcher, and then at Stanley, who nodded encouragingly. It was as if a stinging rush flooded through me at the thought. I looked at the butcher's bloody hands, and I felt a kind of dizziness. But not from aversion or disgust, rather from a sort of, I don't know, a sort of intoxication.

'He gives you the time of one more animal to consider,' the interpreter said, when the butcher fetched another wild boar.

Now I studied him with all the more attention. I was the novice, and I stood there with a feeling of having come to the end of the road. The thought of it filled me with life. I closed my eyes, felt the wind in my hair, suddenly my limbs seemed filled with a strength I was not aware that I possessed, my chest was bursting with a joy I never had thought I would experience. Starry night, and I felt ready. It would be a worthy full stop. The boar that the butcher was preparing for death screamed dreadfully, and I thought that yes, that's how it is, this is all we are, this is all we have, that's why we scream so terribly when we realise it is finally over.

I took the butcher's place, straddled the boar. Before he gave me the knife, he showed me how to cut. I tried, but saw from his expression that he was not impressed.

'He says you must talk to the animal,' the interpreter said. 'Talk calmly.'

'What should I say?' I asked.

'You must think about it as a child,' the interpreter said.

'No, I can't do that,' I said. 'I must think about it as an animal.'

'But think that it is a child who must be calmed,' he said.

'Why?'

'Everyone deserves a painless death,' he says. 'Drive the knife in when the animal has calmed down; then it doesn't get a chance to become scared or feel pain before the whole thing's over.'

I did as he said. I whispered to the boar, as I would have whispered to a child, shushed it, hummed, felt how the little black body kicked, squirmed and wriggled beneath me, and after a few minutes the boar miraculously calmed down, exhausted or reconciled, it was not easy to say. It gave me a sense of great satisfaction. The animal's belly rose and fell more and more slowly, instinctively I felt that the moment had come. I breathed in the weak smell of uric acid, I was completely focused, nothing else existed, it was the animal and me, and then I let the knife fall, hard and fast, penetrating the animal's neck with a short, gurgling suck. For a brief moment the animal jerked beneath me, the blood pumped out of the wound and flooded my hand, warm and stinking. Then I pulled the knife out with a rasping sound, as if I cut through everything there was of veins, airways, fibres and meat, bent the animal's head backwards and cut its throat, at the same time as I pulled the head closer to my chest, until I could hear the bones break in two with dry, resigned cracks. I felt an enormous joy, a kind of jubilation or euphoria which I had never before been even close to feeling. I lifted my arms in the air and threw my head back, looked at the starry sky, Cassiopeia was dim in the far distance, the animal's blood dripped from my hands, Stanley took photographs, the butchers showed restrained sincerity, and it struck me suddenly that all this time I had lived my life in a shadowy existence, in remote corners where the sun never shone, and through my heart's elated beats and the exhilarating roar of my pulse, I could hear myself whisper:

'It is accomplished!'

'Ecce homo,' Stanley mumbled, his eyes shining with admiration.

The butcher stood over me. He smiled approvingly, took my arm and led me over to the bonfire. He lit a joint, took a couple of puffs and gave it to me.

'Well done,' he said. 'We've all got it in us.'

Then he left, and I sent the interpreter away with him. I sat alone at the bonfire. I shivered from sheer rapture. I listened to Boy and his eternal mantra from the rubbish heap, breathed in the smell of cannabis, felt how the bhang gradually calmed me down. New heart-piercing screams ripped through the darkness of the evening. My retina sparkled with stars and embers. No melancholy. I had come to the end of the road, but I didn't feel any sorrow. It was accomplished. This was the most real of all my moments as a human being. And probably the last.

89

At dawn I stood with my feet in the mud, unapproachable in the throng of cripples, unassailable among the lame and the crooked, these people whom nature had mocked with useless bodies. Ganges immense and slumbering before me, the crackling sparks from the cremation pyres, the smouldering ash, the butchery on the other side, where I, the night before, finally, had become complete. The dripping blood that got mixed with the river water and millions of liberated souls. I was high on marihuana. I undressed and stood naked on the river bank with the other naked people. Usha's blush fell over my slim, pale body. I thought about the words of the wise man Badarayana, that Ganges would assist me with the rest. And Ganges, this enormous, dirty whore, was spreading her legs before me, and all I had to do was to walk a few metres and sink into her. But no, it was already accomplished, it had no purpose, I thought, when suddenly someone behind me said my name. I turned slowly around, it was as if my body had enclosed itself around me, I felt the intoxication running like poison or cure through my blood. On the river-bank, in the shade of a palm tree, sat Detective Harding. And I thought: it does.

from COME, COME, LISTEN TO THE NIGHTINGALE

Einar O. Risa

No? I don't know. But he was going to be executed. Ardengo Soffici was circling the paintings. The year was 1909, P. S. Krøyer was done for, he had no clue. Someone was out to destroy him, to strip him of his life, his art and reputation, his honour. He had eaten breakfast at the restaurant of the Hotel Luna, had drunk coffee, had written yet another letter to the White House in Skagen. My dearest Henny, he'd written to Mrs Brodersen, I imagine that you are here, and I hope that my numerous letters do not bring ill will into your household. He was heading towards the exhibition, the Biennale in Venice, to experience the big canvases there, and it was as though Henny walked beside him down the street, he could talk with her, show her. His paintings filled two halls. Here was his life, here were the paintings, here was *Sankt Hans Blus på Skagen Strand*, his most recent large painting, all his friends, his admired Marie, the most beautiful woman in Denmark, and Hugo Alfvén, the snake from the Garden of Eden who had stolen her from him, and Henny, of course, looking directly at him, the painter, just as he wanted her to, while the others were looking at the bonfire, all the artists at Skagen gathered on the beach, Holger Drachmann, Anna Ancher, Michael Ancher, Laurits Tuxen, and then all the others in the bonfire's flickering light: Degn Brøndum, the city treasurer Hans Brodersen, Vibeke, his own and Marie's Vipsen. All in one painting, and it was finished, it was true. He could see it before him, on the wall. He'd worked on this painting year after year. It had stood untouched in his atelier at Krøyer's House in Skagen throughout his illness, until he'd been able to lift the brush again. Two halls with his paintings. Here was the large blue painting, in the evening light, the painter P. S. Krøyer, his wife Marie and the dog Rap, *Sommeraften ved Skagen Strand*, painted only ten years before, in another life, so removed, here were *Italienske Landsbyhattemagere, Et Sardineri I Concernau, Badende Drenge en Sommeraften ved Skagen Strand.* He'd filled wall after wall, 24 paintings, and he'd been one of the five chosen for the international Biennale in Venice this spring. He stood in there, inside, alone, and it was true, P. S. Krøyer had aged quickly. It was apparent now, looking at him, old, yet no more than 58 come summer. Illness and hospitalisation had left their marks in his eyes, on his face, his stooped body. Was the young Ardengo Soffici mocking him? Shaking his head over this relic of a man who could no longer keep up, whose time had passed without him having noticed. Why had P. S. Krøyer travelled the long way to the Biennale in Venice? The paintings were more than enough. Was it his last, awkward curtain call for the world? Nearly blind behind his spectacles, yet here none the less, and Ardengo Soffici was going to execute him. It had been planned. It would make the front page of *La Voce*. Soffici would stand right behind him, would watch him squinting at his own paintings, only to turn and nearly stumble into Soffici without knowing who he'd nearly stumbled into, mumbling something unintelligible, and Soffici might suddenly think: does he know after all? Could he have heard rumours? Will even the milliner be mocked? Does he know that it will be written about in *La Voce*, that it will cover the front page, attract attention? And that it was possible for Krøyer to hear Ardengo Soffici's mocking laughter all the way from his regular table at the Guibbe Rosse in Florence, from before he'd left, Ardengo Soffici had known what he would write and that it would be noticed, *La Voce* would be a periodical that people discussed, the new voices, the future, and Ardengo Soffici had gone to the Biennale in Venice to cleanse the museums, to clear away, to make room, all these decrepit old men who'd been passed by, yes, that's it, passed by, they didn't understand the meaning of momentum. Ardengo Soffici wandered from room to room taking notes, he would write yet another article, he would fill many issues of *La Voce* with his analyses, he would take them on, one after the other, these decrepit old men, Franz von Stuck, Anders Zorn, Albert Besnard, Ettore Tito, P. S. Krøyer. Ardengo Soffici walked from painting to painting viewing them with disgust, he would note yet another caustic remark in his notebook, this foolishness, this art that was not art, but an assertion to art, painted with sponges, wiped across the canvas with the awareness of what the public wants, knowing what the indolent critics want to find at an exhibition, Ardengo Soffici took notes, he would put them all in their place. And I am there, in the pen that gnaws its way over the page, it is so familiar, yet another bit of sarcasm, was he satisfied, this young Ardengo Soffici? He had turned thirty in the spring, he'd returned home to Florence with new ideas, in Paris he'd seen the Cubists, he'd met Georges Braque, André Derain, Pablo Picasso, Juan Gris and he'd wanted more, he'd painted, he'd written, articles, poems, and he had a novel in his head, and so many texts, commentaries, a whole series of articles from the Venice Biennale, he wandered through the halls, he could have sidled up alongside P. S. Krøyer and Krøyer wouldn't have had any idea who he was, no, he couldn't, Ardengo Soffici would have been just one of the many people who positioned themselves in front of the big paintings, just another young stranger standing there in front of the painting of the poor, sweaty Italian milliner, studying the drop that hung under the man's nose, just a tiny thing, he had thought, a drop under the man's nose, and P. S. Krøyer is a famous artist, Ardengo Soffici noted, this he could use, he looked at the painting, indifferent as a graveyard, he thought, he wrote.

HE CAN'T REMEMBER. HE GOES ASHORE

1888. He came to Stavanger, and he might have been someone else. Did it come from here, all of it? It must have been inside him. In his head, his brain, his eyes, his fingers. Who looked when he looked? Who painted with his strokes? Who was he? Peder Severiin Gjesdahl? He had worked on *Hip, Hip, Hurra!*, the friends' feast. He wasn't finished. He'd been working on the painting for many years, it had slipped from his grasp again and again. He travelled back to Norway. He was 37 years old and he'd been a Danish citizen for less than two years. P. S. Krøyer stood on deck. The steamship glided in toward the harbour, toward the quay. The visit wouldn't be a long one, only a day and a half. The steamship pulled into the quay, the hawser was thrown ashore, the boat moored, he could see the town square, the cathedral at the crest of the small hill, the Kielland house in front of the lake called Bredevannet. He couldn't see the asylum for the indigenous and the insane, Den kombinerede Indretning, it was hidden behind the rows of houses.

This was Stavanger.

He had been here before. He couldn't remember it. He went ashore, he walked over the town square, he had planned to spend the night in the town, to visit Alexander L. Kielland. P. S. Krøyer stood in front of the door, waiting and was disappointed. Kielland had gone to the farmland of Jæren. Yet again he had travelled from the town, to the place he couldn't do without, Orre.

Well, if that was where he was, then he would have to visit him out there by the sea!

*

But I certainly found much to see in Stavanger, P. S. Krøyer wrote in a letter. He had something to tell his mother, his real mother in Copenhagen. Stavanger is beautiful and quite charming. The town, with its many old herring warehouses, was very picturesque, he wrote.

Nothing about the asylum.

Could that be picturesque?

To him? To Peder Severin Krøyer, born Gjesdahl.

In this town.

How would he manage to find something?

Could there be anything other than evasion and silence?

The first thing we did was go to the cathedral. They have done extensive renovations, he could write to her, and he could buy a postcard for his mother, a photograph of the town as it had become since she'd left it, a photograph to show her how the town had changed.

The old cathedral hadn't changed, it was still there, at the top of the town square. The cathedral's papers were there, the church register was there, he was in it, one name among many names, born to Elen Cecilie Gjesdahl the 23rd July 1851, Peder Severiin, as he'd been spelled out, and illegitimate.

It is a very beautiful church, both the interior and exterior, he was able to write in the letter she was waiting for.

Nothing about the mystery of the church register.

Who was he? The man Peder Severiin?

Illegitimate.

That's what he was.

A result. His mother, institutionalised at the asylum, mentally ill, she hadn't been able to care for herself, she had to be cared for by others, and some, no, not someone, a man took care of her when she couldn't take care of herself, and that resulted in a child. Was it the child of Niels Iversen Solberg Hjorth, the superintendent for the indigent? As it is written in the church register, Superintendent for the Indigent N. S. Hjorth and the maiden Elen Cecilie Gjesdahl?

There were rumours in town, in the streets, whispers about the baby, that it couldn't be the superintendent, no, it wasn't him, he only gave his name for the child to use, that was all, and then they whispered, no, oh no, could it be true? Him? Could it be? Well, yes. Yes. But? The rumours swirled in the little town on the western coast, the whispering, was he the one? No, there is someone else, it is that one, and then the name, and then another. No, no. It can't be true. From mouth to ear, in the square, outside the Kielland residence, in the harbour, in front of the cathedral, speculations but no answers, only all these speculations. No, it can't be? While she was committed? Oh my, what's the world coming to?

Sigh.

That horrible place.

He didn't write about that, he wrote about something else. He went to Bredevannet and to Kongsgaarden, the old school that stood unchanged, but for the addition of a new wing erected a few years earlier, he can tell her that, and he chanced upon the rector himself, the renowned rector Steen, left-wing politician and parliament member, who escorted Peder Severin Krøyer around the school, showing him the old monks' chapel, which housed the school's library, showing him old schoolrooms, which stood just as they had in the old days.

Peder Severiin can tell his mother in Copenhagen: the old Kongsgaard garden has been opened as a public park and the trees are so tall that you can only see the very top of the cathedral's steeple from the opposite side of the lake. After that we sought out Kielland, who lives in his mother's old house, just beside Kongsgaard's garden, which faces the lake, but, as I said, he wasn't in. So we walked around Bredevannet and up the street called Ladegaardsveien. The whole hillside, where you used to ride your sled in the old days, Kjelkebakken, the Sled Hill, is now completely covered with houses, some of them charities or endowment projects. On the other side of the lake, just in front of the cathedral, they've also constructed buildings. Among other things, they've built a railway station for the line to Egersund. Afterward we walked to the quayside, Vågen, and drove out to Ladegaardsveien to a hilltop called Vaalandshøyden, where we had a lovely view over the whole region that you know so well. That hill belongs to the Kielland family. From there one has a good view of Ledaal. On the way there we drove along the lake Hillevaagsvannet, through Hillevaag. From there we had to take a train to Jæderen, where we were greeted with open arms by Kielland and his family. Their house is right on the shoreline in a landscape that is very like Skagen and Jylland. There we ate a late lunch and took great pleasure in one another's company.

Had I met Kielland in Stavanger, I would have seen much more of Stavanger and had a measure of news that would have been of interest to you. As it is, you will have to make due with the image on the photograph and what it can tell you of Stavanger's appearance today.

So much Kielland could have shown him, told him.

*

P. S. Krøyer, and he might have been some other, had he never been sent away to Copenhagen, he might have been the typographer who woke suddenly and was too late, terrified in the dark and February's cold, the paper! thought the typographer, the newspaper, what would the editor Kielland say? The paper had to be finished, it couldn't be finished without him, without his lightning-quick fingers over the die-cases, letter for letter, line for line, column for column. The newspaper wouldn't be a newspaper until he was there and could receive Kielland's long, hand-written articles and transform them into yet another article for the Stavanger newspaper, and the readers, friends, foes could read what the horrible Kielland had concocted now, he waved a whip over the town, he was a joy for the country, he'd written it himself, dipped his pen in ink and written, word for word, and now it has been changed into a newspaper, and the typographer had read it along the way, sneering behind a mask, finally someone speaks out, loud and clearly, and so, now he was running late, a new article was to be printed and he had to hurry, quick, quick down the stairs with his braces flailing behind him like a tail on which he could stumble, but he didn't stumble, he gathered his tail and fastened it, button by button to his trousers, and then to this day, this morning that should turn the town on its head, because Kielland has got it worked out now, he's been walking around for days, collecting fodder for the first article on the asylum, Den kombinerede Indretning, he's been there, knocked and demanded to enter, he wanted to see it himself, he didn't want to write only about the rumours, he had walked through one room after the other, through the mental ward, the indentured labour areas, the hospital, he had seen it, he had experienced the stench there and heard the howling and the laughter and the screams. He had written. Pen and ink, page after page. And now there would be a newspaper, and the typographer ran through the dark streets, through the long Strandgaten and hadn't tied his shoes, ran over the cobblestones, along the quayside, passed the night watchman, through the square and into the office, and there was the editor Kielland, and he was restless, the article was ready, it had to be set, and the typographer's fingers flew over the case of type, letter by letter, and the first page of the Stavanger newspaper, Thursday, 7th February 1889, took form, he could read while the type fell into place, the mirror image, he could read the chastising editor Kielland addressing the asylum's misery, let us first try to get an overview of the kind of misery it is that attends this asylum, in which highly distinct forms of human suffering are packed in together behind these common walls and under these shared executors. First are the dangerous transients, violent gangs and questionable characters who stem from every part of the country and from Sweden, and here are the helpless old women in the so-called 'house of corrections' waiting for death, then we have the female population of the workhouse, insane women, disreputable and impossible mothers and wives, together they form an endless train of mad girls who created mischief and disruption in the town, and housed with these are all the town's ill, people who can't be cared for at home, people who have been injured, are infectious, servant girls and other homeless, poor men and women with all kinds of diseases, with a disproportionate number of syphilis cases.

And then in the middle of all this, a lunatic asylum!

Yes, why not?

The one doesn't appear to be madder than the other, that is, an ancient depository for the crazy, which is always overflowing. So why not add another function or two for the asylum, a public bath, a public restaurant with a smokehouse, a laundry, a mortuary, a stonemason's workshop, then one has an idea of what the Stavanger kombinerede Indretning is.

His fingers flew over the type.

The typographer exhaled, wiped the sweat from his forehead, leaving black streaks on his face.

The newspaper has taken form. It has been finished.

And finally a cup of steaming, black coffee.

It could have easily been him.

*

Only silence. Not a word. Not the words. The riddle. Who he was. He might have been some other. He might have stood in the town square selling fish or vegetables. He might have stood behind the counter in one of the shops, he might have been a cooper and made barrels for the fishermen, for the factory workers, for Bjelland. Or a carpenter down on the quayside wharf. Or why not a night watchman, and he might have walked through the nights, through the streets of Stavanger, up to Valberget, and he might have had the town below him, and it would have been his town, he'd have watched over it, that there'd be no fire tonight.

Who might he have been? He was in Stavanger, he had wandered around the town, had he seen himself? There? That may have been him? That boy? He looked in the town square, along the harbour, the cathedral, Bredevannet, he strolled through the narrow streets. The town wasn't large, the cathedral was only a few hundred metres from the asylum. Did he dare? Did he walk there? Stop outside the gate? Did he hear the calls from inside, the noise? Was it tempting? Open the door, here was the beginning, in here, in one of the rooms, in the darkness through which he stumbled? Which door? Who could he ask? Could he ask? Did he dare? Did he push the thought away? Pull away from the unpleasantness? Did he walk a different route? Not there, no, not there.

Who was he?

His mothers hadn't told him.

They knew that he wanted to know.

There isn't an explanation. They wouldn't speak.

Perhaps it was only shame. A lifelong shame. And he was the shame. He was there, with his eyes, his gaze, the open mouth, the words that were said and those that never passed the lips, only a sudden silence.

The two mothers. The Gjesdahl sisters.

*

Now you have to keep the peace. Have you chased her off again? Your sister? The woman who followed you to Copenhagen. Has she moved yet again, how many apartments can she have lived in, in Nørrebro? Always there, in that area.

No peace.

They tore in him. Each from their side, as with rasping claws, and he couldn't escape his mothers. They both wanted him, wanted him exclusively.

He pulled away, held back, avoided them, he changed the subject, he painted picture after picture and they hungered for the credit.

He is my son.

He is my son.

Can you please get along?

And then the suffocating silence.

They talked and talked.

They didn't say a word.

Who was he?

THE EMPTY TABLE. PARTY

He held on to his painting tightly, showing it around, it was his. There they were gathered. He was there himself, beaming, flushed and laughing, in the midst of a call of *Hip, Hip,* poised for *Hurrah*! He directed the whole gathering with his left hand, his index finger extended, and a glass of champagne in the other hand. This is how it should be, in the shade of the trees, in the light sunshine that hits the leaves, that pushes through the foliage here and there, lighting up faces, shining in eyes, on a light dress, on a white dinner jacket, in the lifted glasses. It is summer, it is Skagen. In the garden the table is set, bottles of champagne are opened and the dinner is coming towards an end, there will be a toast, and the men have stood, raised their arms, glasses of champagne in their hands, bubbling champagne, *Hip, Hip,* and the arm is directing, *Hurrah*! The women remain seated, there are three of them, the one easily recognisable, it is Anna Ancher with the crooked nose, she's holding a bored child set to run off, twisting in her mother's dress, aren't they finished yet? It is Helga Ancher, with the fair hair, in a white summer dress, and Anna Ancher looks down at her, mouth open, cut off in a *Hip, Hip,* and she says something to Helga, yes, yes, soon now, then you can go play. Or else the opposite, Helga has just come to the grown-ups' table and is grabbing Anna's dress, holding fast, while she swings her left foot over the bench to sit with them, and Anna Ancher says, all right, all right, just a little while with us, then it will pass, whatever it was, Helga comes suddenly running through the garden, excited, hurried, she has to tell her something. Next to Anna Ancher sits Helene Christensen, she has lifted her champagne glass, she looks toward the standing men, she looks across the table to the other side where Søren is standing with an open mouth, in the middle of his *Hip, Hip, Hurrah!* He is the person she is looking at, her Søren, because he is the one, he had seen her and he paid no mind to her slight limp, her petite stature, that she was only a schoolmistress, and he was the fantastic Søren, the festive Søren, the laughing and smiling Søren, he saw her, and here she sits, in the fine, warm summer, in the playful flecks of sunshine under the trees, she sees him, turned from Anna, she sees Søren. Does he see her? Through the glass of the lorgnette?

Yes, yes, one can imagine that she's the one he's looking to, that it is to her he is lifting his glass at this moment. They toast. Martha Johansen doesn't join the toast. She has only just lifted her glass from the table and she doesn't look up at the standing men, her eyes are focused in front of her, down towards the festively decorated table. Søren has painted her from behind, bending forward slightly, leaning towards the table covered with the white tablecloth. Is it a point of contention? Because Martha can't stop talking long enough to keep up? She speaks her mind, she's not a bohemian, how would she have the time to live the life of a lusty artist? She cares for the children, she helps her Viggo so that he can have the time and space to paint, she is also his model, she has enough to do, and they don't live at the artists' colony, they keep their distance, Martha and Viggo, she keeps a distance for them both. And there she sits, alone at the end of the table, and the men toast each other, they don't look to her, they toast each other, cheers Viggo Johansen, cheers Christian Krohg, cheers Søren Krøyer, cheers Degn Brøndum, cheers

Michael Ancher, cheers Oscar Björck, cheers Thorvald Niss, and Thorvald Niss leans over the table, in high spirits, arm extended, his glass with less liquid than the others, he had to have a taste, he couldn't wait, ah, that was lovely, and then he toasts, *Hip, Hip,* and *Hurrah!*

It has never happened.

FROM I DON'T GO OUT ANY MORE, I HOVER OVER THE CITY
Einar O. Risa

I don't go out any more, he wrote. There was a last time, and I can see the tracks through the city, on the dry asphalt, on the cobblestones, along the sidewalks, the morphine lifts me up and I hover over the streets, over my own tracks down Fiolstræde, Krystalgade, through Arnold Busck's bookstore, along Klareboderne, and I can see that I have stopped in front of Bo-Bi Bar, in front of the window, to peer in before I opened the door, and I have continued on to Kongens Nytorv, the King's square, where it is suddenly as warm as August, but I don't perspire, I glide on the mild current of air that has finally reached us from Europe, from Italy, past Germany, I hover over the city and I hear the voices from below, a woman talking on her mobile phone, she has stopped at the entrance to the metro, she says she has been delayed, but is on her way, yes, she's coming, and then she disappears down the stairs, and I can't see her any longer, can't hear her, but she is waiting for the train to arrive, for the doors to open on to the platform, the train's doors will open, while another voice rises above the din, yet another woman, and a man, no, she's told him, they walk through the square, towards Gothersgade, they go into Kongens Have, where they find a bench and sit, he puts his arm around her shoulders but she pulls back, moves slightly away from him, no, she says again, and so they sit there, on the bench, barely visible beneath the trees, I hover over them, over the city's rooftops and towers I hover, over the parliament building, over Tøger Seidenfaden who sits in his office in the newspaper *Politiken*, stooped and sweaty and more than a little annoyed, over yet another editorial on the desk of the political editor, he writes and I glide on, I won't be able to read what he's writing, it's none of my business now, I hover over Gammel Kongevej, near the pavement now, so that I can see Fredericksberg Antiquarian Bookshop, which is going out of business just like me, I can see my footprints in front of the shop window, I have lingered there, too, I have looked inside and allowed myself to give in to the temptation to open the door, because I hadn't been able to resist the leather-bound edition of *Salmonsen's Big Illustrated Encyclopaedia, A Nordic Encyclopaedia. With the Contribution of Librarian J. B. Halvorsen, Chief Editor for Norway, and nearly 200 Nordic Experts and Scientists*, edited by *Chr. Blangstrup*. I can see myself taking one of the books from the shop window, ignoring the woman behind the counter and her frown, but she doesn't say anything, she doesn't get up, and I lift the heavy volume, it's volume III (Bischarin–Canada), dated Copenhagen 1894, and I can't help but leaf through it, Boom, the city in the Belgian province Antwerp, near the Brussels canal with its mouth in the Rupel, over which hangs a beautiful bridge, or Boom [bu!m], Jan van, Dutch musician, born 1807 in Utrecht, died 1872 in Stockholm, and then about Boom, the musician, the composer . . . his compositions are of no value independently, he was, however, a gifted piano teacher. His brother, Herman v. B. (1809–93) functioned as an excellent flautist in his native country. Signed W. B., it is Behrend, W., Cand. Jurist, Attorney at Law. And I can't help myself. I have to find volume II, find B, Behrend, W., but there is no Behrend, W., only a Behrend, Heinrich Theodor, German politician and grain merchant, born 1817, who had been forced to step down from public service when Merchant House B. went bankrupt. I can see myself being consumed by these concentrated lives, and there I stand, by the window of the second-hand bookseller's, Fredericksberg Antiquarian Bookshop, receiving several more suspicious glances from the woman behind the counter, guarding her encyclopaedia, and I give in to temptation, it's irresistible, I have to have these metres of knowledge, these fragments of the world edited by Chr. Blangstrup, it can't be put off, and I buy it, all of it, from the flabbergasted woman behind the counter, and I ask her to call a taxi for me so that I can get them home to Classensgade, and she reluctantly dials a number, and then a car comes and stops outside the door of Fredericksberg Antiquarian Bookshop and the driver rolls his eyes at the mountain of books I carefully carry outside and put in his back seat while he watches, shaking his head imperceptibly, I can see it in his eyes, I carry the last of the volumes into the car, placing them carefully next to all the others, it will be fine, I sigh, perspiring from lifting the books, they won't fall out, I say to the taxi driver, and he shakes his head, perceptibly this time, but I'm not certain, it could happen anyway, a sudden turn, near Triangeln, for example, the car door might open, book after book falling on to the asphalt, in the middle of the street, and a bus, it could be number 15 with its double-decker bulk, rumbling over my newly purchased books, my encyclopaedia transformed into useless, filthy paper with the tracks of giant rubber tyres. Shredded. It could happen. I sit beside the driver, Classensgade, I say, and he pulls out on to Gammel Kongevej, and I can see the trail I've left behind and the trail of my encyclopaedia through the city, where I hover away, over H. C. Ørstedsvej, over Nørrebro, just beyond Assistens Cemetery and down Blegedamsvej, past the General Hospital towards Trianglen, over Østerbrogade past Sortedams Lake, and then left just before reaching Lille Triangel, turning on to Classensgade, and soon I'll be able to continue my journey through the letter B, because I don't go outside any more, wrote Hans Kanne in one of the notes that lay on the desk in his white iBook.

Come, said Hans Kanne. I didn't go, I don't know why, it just wasn't
convenient then, there was something else, a job, yet another deadline. But I did go, later, and am sitting on his couch with a dark
November-morning view of the city, it's quiet now after the night's
intense rain against the windows, thunder and blinking lightning all
over the city. I write. I have been here before, this is the fourth time
this year, the plane from Stavanger has come in over Jylland, I have
seen Skagen and Grenen, to the left, far below me, Århus, and then
Copenhagen, a turn over Øresund Bridge, another landing at Kastrup
airport. During the first visit, which was only six months ago, he'd
shown me Hammershøi. You've got to see this, he'd said, then, sitting
in his penthouse apartment on Classensgade, six floors up with no
elevator, but worth the work to get up all the stairs, five rooms, far
too much space for him, we sat in the living room and looked out
over the roofs and spires of Copenhagen, towards the sound, the
ferries coming and going, the windmills turning lazily in the May
breeze out there, Sweden lay right behind them, Skåne, Malmö.

I can sit here for hours just looking out over the city, I couldn't
do that before, he said. And then he spoke of Hammershøi, when I
look at that painting I understand that I made the wrong career
choice, he said, words, words, what are they? Nothing when I stand
in front of this painting.

He drove me out to Ordrupgaard.

It wasn't that he wanted to show me all the empty rooms, dust and light, a woman painted from behind, nearly always the same woman, there was something else, a big painting, dark, five men who stare at us.

Look, he said without saying more, he stood there, silent, stood there like that for a long while, and then turned toward me.

Coffee? he asked, there is a café in the park.

I wanted to see the other paintings.

I'll wait outside, he said, he didn't want to see them, he had seen them, he said, many times, he had come here only to see the one painting, it had come to this now, he said later, I can't stand museums, pictures piled one on top of the other, the one distorting the other. I choose just one and then I come back only to see that one. This is how I will use my time.

He must have known then, but he hadn't said anything, he didn't say anything later, either, when we were back at his apartment sitting in front of the big living room window looking out over the roofs and the spires, and not when we sat at Bo-Bi Bar, at the table by the window just beside the front door with a view to Gyldendal's gate across the street, and not later still when we sat at Palæ Bar listening to jazz recordings in the background, Chet Baker, Billie Holiday, Bill Evans above the buzz of conversation, and he drank Limfjords Porter.

You have to taste this, he said, rope and seaweed in a bottle, he sneered.

I tasted it and chose a wheat beer instead.

He didn't say anything when I'd returned home and we spoke on the telephone, not when he asked me if I would come down to visit again, either.

You and your news, he said, find something else.

Yeah, yeah, I said, later.

It may be too late, he said, laughing into the receiver, they might run out of Limfjords Porter.

That would be a serious tragedy, I answered.

I have to choose, he told Ann one night, she told me. He put it like that. I have to choose. I don't have any more time. Should I read *Berlin Alexanderplatz* or should I read *Hunger* one last time? Or should I see a film? His voice was so weak, it was late in the evening and I was about to go to bed, but I couldn't, Ann said. He wanted to talk, and the telephone was so quiet.

What should I choose, he asked, I am so tired but I can't sleep, he said, I've gone for a walk, he said, a long walk in the library, I've gathered books.

But I have to choose, he said again, and he was annoyed, how can I possibly choose? I don't want to, I don't want to, he said, and I could hear him throw a book to the floor, said Ann.

He sat in the office with the stacks of books on both sides of his chair. I shouted to him and he didn't answer, only breathed heavily, he put down the phone receiver, I heard it hit the table, I don't know what he'd done, I didn't hear anything, and then the laboured breathing, as though he were trying to take a deep breath, but couldn't. I heard him inhale through his mouth, I had heard him like this before and it was unpleasant. I called to him again, I called several times and he didn't answer. I waited and waited and then he finally picked up the receiver.

Did you think I'd gone somewhere? he asked. No, no, not yet, not yet, he repeated and then his voice faded. No, he said, or whispered, rather weakly. And then with greater strength, as though he'd pulled himself together, no.

Silence again, I heard him pick up a book, leafing through the pages.

No, he whispered again, not that one and then I could hear him slide the book across the floor. He picked up another, or maybe sat there with several books in his lap. *Trees that fall*, he mumbled, *Extinction*, yes, I can't manage it, but I can hold it in my hand, I can look at the cover, I can read the first lines, and just remember, remember.

I could hear him put the books aside, I could hear that he was bending over to pick up others, the chair made a noise, the leather creaked. *The Boathouse*, he whispered, *Black Banners*, you remember, the first page, I will never forget. Beckett? Simon, you would like it, wouldn't you, if I chose Simon, if I sat here again with *The Acacia*? You'd like that?

I could hear a pile of books tumble.

Swift, he mumbled. Not that one, he shouted.

I don't know which book he'd picked up, he didn't say. But I heard him send another book sliding across the floor.

Which should I choose? he shouted with a broken, hoarse voice, which should I choose? he asked me, barely audible now.

What could I answer?

Ann looked over at me.

What could I have answered? she said again.

FROM **THE COMING YEARS**
Øyvind Rimbereid

UP DOWN

It's the throbbing pain that chases us. Whoosh, whoosh, away with us! Down the stairs, out the door and quick around the corner. In between the garages and down the stony path towards the lawn and the playground. There's nothing else we can do, my boy and I. No one can fight against that burning pain. Although we do, even so. Precisely when we chase ourselves out – either a trip in the car, or most often just down to the playground. Call at the shop first, Cola for Stig and a magazine for me. If we don't see any young people before entering the shop, Stig can have a mag, too. Of course. Stig can't play football with me. Johs can do that. Instead, I give him a push on the swings. Mostly, though, we sit on a bench, read and stare. Up at the block of flats, at the window with the closed green curtains. Though our block isn't all that big, it's easy to see the curtains. Those that hang in front of the room where the burning pain is at work. How long do we have to wait? How many hours do we have to sit here this time? Perhaps someone I know will come along, and a couple of lads Stig can play football with. It's the pottering, talking moments that can stretch time out, but never shut off. We can't help ourselves. Now perhaps? we think and stare up at the block of flats. We don't know it. It's not us it talks to. The gnawing way it speaks no one else is able to hear. It runs up from the back of the neck, grating in every direction, every convolution. In there where it hangs out it is all that exists. That is why we have to chase it away. 'Can hardly face the thought that anyone exists,' Johs says from his bed, in a low voice and with his old scarf over his eyes. It's the blue scarf he uses when it comes at its worst. 'The cool colour,' he says. 'Keeps things out better.' Behind it, it can burn and throb away in peace, burn itself out. How long will he need some peace this time? Two days? Five? No way we can tell. Or do anything. We've just got to let it do its work. We've got to manage this. This this. We've nothing to complain about. Apart from this one thing, that it keeps on coming. For a week or two it's as if it's been blown away. But we're fooled each time. By the secret thing among the convolutions in there, the grating thing that can't be mended. And we're being chased, in separate directions, Johs there, we here. By something so simple. The one thing that morning. Sometimes I can see it in my mind's eye. How it fell, so long and so long a time – it fell in an endlessly long spiral, that crowbar. We can't help. What will it do with us? Where will we go with it? Where are we going this evening? We won't be in the square, won't take the car, won't be visiting. This evening we'll walk among the trees. Walk through the park and can already see the fair they've rigged up at the end. Red, violet. The sounds spreading out. Whining, wailing towards us. We can't always just sit still, keep our mouths tight shut and glue our feet to the floor. Not so easy to disappear from under Johs's nose when we're in the same house. The house can't be big enough for him! While *they* say: you won't be short of space at any rate, no matter what, it will be an insurance there somewhere. 'If things go well for us, the money will pour in,' the federal lawyer said to us here recently. Didn't he give a little smile when he said that, I wonder? We've got 40,000 already, plus a greeting from the managing director. 'And there'll be more, if things should turn out *that* bad.' *That* bad? We don't want them – damages for pain and suffering. Even if we actually end up getting them. 'Yes, and even if we might happen to need them!' said Johs yesterday, lying with his neck sticking out the side of the bed. To find the angle, as he put it. The angle where breaks can come. Is he having a break now? Behind the curtains, behind the eyes? Quivering, as I see they are at night. It's the black, burning part they look into. He's got his own burning light. While the lights at the end of the park are for everyone. Red, violet. Johs is still able to go to work. From time to time, for a couple of days. But never out in the local area. He sits in the office, takes the phone and shows people the way who come with equipment. It's the safety deputy who's fixed that. He's on Johs's side. He defends the pain, the place pain has when it can't be remedied, can't be driven back. It may start coming in waves, we've been told. Long, loose waves that spread out over the weeks, months. Perhaps at some point they will be like ripples, glittering flecks out there? Like the lights behind the fence we can see down there ahead. Out of the park, across the gravel. The tea-cups spin, the antennae on the dodgem cars crackle with sparks. People come towards us with popcorn and candy floss. What a noise, what lights! Stig can forget himself as he flies off. Even though Johs is lying there back home, full of himself, trapped by all that burning, burning. It sometimes makes me think of all the prisoners that exist, that have to sit inside all the time. How often mustn't they try in their minds to move things, to float out of themselves? In a magazine I was looking at the other day up in the sorting office, I read that some of them seemed to speak in tongues. Their thoughts 'ran wild', it said. We must have a go on the dodgems, and the mirrors in the flat, red house. And the big dipper that twists and turns so high up above everything. We must go up in that, too. We don't listen to those people that say you must wait with things. We don't listen either to Stig's aunt, who's always phoning. 'She only does it for the best,' Johs mumbles. The best for who, for what? For God? Because he was the one who dropped that crowbar and now wants to ask for forgiveness? Good god, all is forgiven! That mercy Johs's sister says can come through faith, and that will turn the darkness into light, doesn't need to be as big as she wants it to be. Basically, we want it to be *small*, it ought to be almost *nothing*. Just that small thing, that one thing, that fell for so long and must have gleamed so white ... It was a Tuesday, it had been raining and I was taking a cigarette break with Hanne. Hanne said that her daughter had finally begun to pull her socks up at school. That was when they came into the canteen. They said it was the phone. I remember remember. The poster with a mountain on it, the way over to the taxi. Was I pushing the B post into the sorting office when it fell? No, no great mercy! It's just that it perhaps is still falling, still hasn't swerved in and down. The cars glide above our heads. People laugh and scream. Out in the dark, out in the evening their voices disappear. If Johs had gone blind, he would have been able to be with us here, heard, felt. All this that is not him himself and that constantly pulls him inwards. Then I could have led him in among the stalls and people. Down into the car with us. But Johs isn't blind! I can't lead him off, lead him to the car Stig's already sitting in. On with the seat belt. Rattling we rise. Towards the mountain the mountain before the valley the valley. We see trees, rooftops, the lake far below us. But Johs isn't going to *die*! I feel like saying every time Johs' sister talks the way she does. Even though it can happen, when it feels like it's weeks since I've seen him on his feet – he just goes on lying there in his bedroom. What a stupid idea that worms its way into me then! In the dark convolutions inside his head, broken into two or ten thousand pieces, there is something that simply makes him *more* alive. Johs who can't get away! It smells of wood and burnt sausages. Johs at home under the scarf can't stand smells like that. Beneath us, people wander around as if they want to sample everything, as if there is nothing they don't want to try out, nothing that can't be tried out. In every kiosk, every queue there is something that can happen. Pull the lever and the money comes gushing out – or will next time, perhaps. It's no big deal. Here money vanishes with such joy. Now we can almost see everything here – we glide away on the top of all this humming and rattling. The houses, the streets, the lake. We can see the bay, too. The bay with banners on the ships and boats. As if they are imitating a bygone age where they lie. That's ridiculous! It's not our age, not 1998. The houses on the slope have orange electric lights. Row upon row across the ridge on the other side of the bridge. The gleaming little one in every home. Why can't the dead exist *there* either? Inside the tungsten of the tungsten filament? Or in the screeching sound of the wheels under the cars that in a moment's time will carry us out and down? Everything moves so slowly! And I think so fast! It's as if there was time for everything up here. Also for thinking about Johs's sister, about her mercy. No, how on earth can we think about ourselves in a place like this? On such an evening? The clouds are green and flat. No birds. We're all going to move now, be flung out and down in the cars and maybe Johs is taking a break, for one tiny glimpse while he is flung out and no longer is Johs behind the curtains, but little little mercy while we all plunge into the evening, which simply receives us.

STAVANGER
Øyvind Rimbereid

In the middle of this Sunday-
time I get off. The bus with young people
 youth on its way, the film by Steven Spielberg,
everything further in disappears into white, yellow wooden houses,
small gardens, the lawns green. And I, older,
am left behind in low sun and the music
from a radio The Beatles' 'Something', trying to divide
the world, divide my life between what exists
and what people must have dreamt.
 What sort of a rift is it I can see?
I am at high Eastertide, sun on the roof tiles,
cars with skis, plastic sledges. Garage doors are open,
as if an auction was about to be held, people leaving
for good, off to Canada and no name, no
story here left behind . . .
 Today white clouds
above the city's seven or nine high-rises, two built by a council

chairman,
later minister, engineer-
contractor with a heart for the heavy but safe
promises into the innermost
of this world.
Are these streets where the dream of the past
has become real, is finally welcomed? Am I standing
among houses where all images of the
future have been taken home? Beneath a southwest-lit
sky lies the city and, outside, mile after mile of
fields, stones, bare rock-face

the sea.
Practically everything I've experienced, I've experienced
here
or in a geography not far removed. The landscape
and the city crisscrossed in each other
and in me and my friends. As if all of
us were enclosed in
all this openness.

But nothing outside?
The hard times of the twenties and thirties, the flight from
hunger,
home to new hunger, the enthusiasm for the Nazis
suddenly over. Later the hidden wars, the silent
slow ones, at the end of my street communists lived
and the many who were far too thirsty
in narrow high-rise wooden houses, the origin
of the name given them, 'The Nigger'
now forgotten.
I don't remember either,
or can only just remember
someone playing punk
two blue car lights, the wound in a hand . . .
It is as if the rays of history

have stumbled, have fallen back
into their first gleam!
How still the streets are
on such holidays. The houses wait
for those walking from room to room, talking on the phone,
watching TV, thinking about work, about the following
day, a following year.
We've got what we need,
everything . . .
except a zoo! where an otter, yes an otter
would have twisted its glistening body through the cool water
of the pool, from the secret hidden depths, a dark shadow
up and on, a piercing Red Indian gaze penetrating our own . . .
Like the Jesus we once
loved (and who one day slid in the oil). But
who we never loved too much, never as strongly,
heavily, painfully that the light of the world wasn't white
enough for her! Our song, never as loud that
it gripped us, ripped us up
or down. Our light, humming song,
just as far above the rage of all dread
the impossible song of all madness, humming away
and home to the mild, friendly song of
our familiar streets.
What song will one day sound in these streets?
Will there be the street fighting of slumps and downsides
and despair? Among us? Stretched out
on the carpet of a total market economy,
on which we are borne, rocked each one and then free in
further and further in
and finally out.
In its wild flapping round the Våland tower, on the heights
high above the city, where we saw everything as from a roundabout,
Hundvåg, Storhaug, Hillevåg, Ullandhaug

and then the fields, the coast, before once more the city,
Eiganes, Hundvåg. Winds to throw
yourself down in
            to fall asleep in. In its wild flapping we saw them
come, as from an old darkness beneath the tower,
snowing through the April evenings we saw them disappear
away from our stretched sheets,
                        away and out towards all corners of Stavanger
            the black, mysterious souls
we evening after evening wished to catch, we evening
after evening failed to catch . . .
            We live in the outermost, uppermost
suburb. But of what city?
                        In the summer a school band still
crosses the North Sea, with open night-faces
towards the yellow flaring light of the oil-rigs. To Newcastle,
Edinburgh, sometimes even right in to Sheffield, to our half-
brothers
from before 1971 and the warm oil-era.
            But over there, scarcely visible among the cranes
at the empty shipyard,
an angel ascending with wings of steel,
            the inscription: 'You Fool, Why Visit Us: The Horror!
The Horror!'
                        Still we are on our way
            it feels like,
on our way into our own image into our good
our better best years. The supply boat in the harbour chugs
past the NATO frigate furthest out. The pennants
of the Atlantic Hotel flutter in international
colours. And the grass in the gardens grows, grows
                        and grows into the fences.
We live in the innermost
figure. It doesn't prevent me, it hardly prevents
anyone any longer, this city in these middle

years. I write Easter 1998, the crocuses
    are opening. Do I now know what is speaking
here? Do I now know what is not speaking
here? What will never be allowed
        to speak here?
    We are at high Eastertide. The evenings
are getting lighter, a white flickering over the grass
        and around the graves where my grandparents from the sea
lie
and my mother, father, brother
             and I
    one morning will disappear
for ever and again into April's light
evenings. The same lightness of light
and too as if the rain might fall,
    and the darkness,
obliquely in like the rain
above our roofs and our furniture
and above the anoraks
that hang ready.
    Far from all fractions
the yellow paint gleams on the wall, a rake is drawn
through the gravel, the cat on its way across the lawn
    looks at me.
    And I turn round into a yes
        and into a no
    while the bus disappears
in among hundreds of thousands of windows ajar,
ajar for those who soon will be returning home.
    But what kinds of faces will they come with then?
With what kind of change of name will they
carry their backpacks home
        to new days?
    At night the fridge drones
far from our dreams.

I still remember my first knife,
'Made in West Germany'.
It is high Eastertide, there is still snow
on the mountains we can see far away to the east,
we are waiting
we are waiting

FROM **SOLARIS CORRECTED**
Øyvind Rimbereid

The unnamed speaker at the beginning of this 36-page poem lives in the year 2480 on the west coast of Norway. He works as some sort of foreman for machines or robots that repair the pipe system under the sea. His whole life is part of a kind of cooperative organisation that has the name 14.6. Towards the end of the poem, he has to leave his life on land, as 14.6 is to be moved to the bottom of the empty oil wells in the North Sea, where a 'safe' new world is going to be constructed. The original language of the poem is a hybrid of West Norwegian dialect, earlier forms of Norwegian and elements of most of the languages to be found round the North Sea today. It was voted poem of the year by listeners to the Norwegian national radio (NRK), and was awarded the Critics' Prize as the best adult book of the year.

WOT wud i turnd owt lyk
if u kuddev krept fra
yor wereld te ours?
SHAYMFEL, i ges wen
u kum wiv yor imagos
ev our taim, tekno, airlyf
all yor epokaliptikl nicht-mares. OR yor bellissiml draums! NAY
we are. NAY yor imagos! DER
i dwels, in 14.6, wee labors
wiv ours naikid nainofinges,
der ours totl hedfakts, wee labors
pokissimo, 30 mins pr jour. I giv mee
finges a luk, part ev organek 14.6,
but slappisloppi, dems lyk seegrass . . .
SO kud i beg yor wereld
te kumens, te start us up
wuns mor? KUD it!
    SHAYMFEL i bee. SO
        wot wud
uev turnd owt lyk
if wee kuds kreep fra
us te u?

/

AT NICHT dem labors in
mud, mee grabmasheens,
deep undr de wayvs
undr de siddi brigg,
self-organising, repairing hydropypes
wid dems simpl 8-funktionboddis.

DEM are 123 pcs, mee robot-
laborers. 123 x 8 x algoritm
               is dems brayn.
     DEMS kollektiv
brayn is abstrakt
end egsist ownli twikst dem
as twikst A end B
or as twikst en odder human end mee
             wen wee speek.
     DEM nay ken aboot
eech odder. DEM nay ken
aboot thems totl systemlabor,
dems kooperation.
DEM onli kens aboot demselvs
end kennet onli in dems intern, closd feedback-
imago, ergo onli
as robot-eksistens.

/

BUT our own wereld?
     IS it also onli intern?
SUMTYMS i find and see on mee skreen,
see regio Norwg-West.
     pikts tayken fra abuv,
luk et all licht at nicht, spots aftr spots
so ticht end kompleks, fra Krisand te Bergn.
SPOTS ev licht in wun sicht,
as if all hung tigedder. WUN sicht
kleer te kut thru all madder
            end all human lyf.
END de saym if i luk et odder regios,
et odder pikts tayken fra abuv. In Chin, for eks,
ware siddis nay kan bee separaytid,
ware infinit amount of sicht is in licht.

END as if on toppa eech odder,
        in e gigantik pattern,
diffikult te ken wot all sichts are tigedder . . .
        OR dem luks lyk harf muuns,
dis? AS big amount harf muuns
up daun, wid erth undr dem,
wid our erth lyk e dark, infinit
           univrs undr it?
JA, is it dis wee bee?
WUN wereld ev harf muuns?
BUT wot den is our sun?
WOT do we riflekt den,
        harf or hole?

/

SIDDI Stavgersand, siddi myn,
eksist neali nay et all, monni
kenkluud nu. KAN bee it eksist
onli es en auld naym,
           as e simbl ev a siddi?
JA, es if playsis in 2480 stil kud bee wichtig!
STAVGERSAND, e neali
           emti plays
in midflo ev so monni
        sels, organeks, konneks, pow en mishmash ev
lors. BUT 'bjuuti' dem ses bee here,
twixt sand en hy fell.
AS a fynl werd fer dis?
'BJUUTI', de werd det kan bee kartid
evriwea. JA, evriware dems fichts
for de werd 'bjuuti'. IF a plays
        nay hev 'bjuuti'
den deas neali no plays dems fond ev.

HERE bee so big flo ev turists,
fra Asi en Russi ofts, det thruu
en upfells shell travl, te green-
    lyf in WYLD-BJUUTI-PARK-NORWG!
EIN veek undr himml
in fellparks mit fowlis ev seldm typs,
en mayhaps dem orlso see e litl hart,
wot bee sudnli mungst de trees,
wiv such e karm, wundring gays aboot dem?
    IN sun, wind, sno, but ofts onli rayn.
DATS wot dem kum for, betalen for and gets inte.
BETALEN for dem boddi en brayns e
        wirklig plays hev bin!
BUT wot dem thingks
    dem wil end up es!

/

BUT wen mee simpl robots
labors on pyp-
sistm undr see, ofts et nicht
undr muun klar: DEMS totl free!
    KAN robots free bee?
JA, dem kan.
WEN dems dun repaerd e problm deep in sludg,
    neali en imposibl problm,
en i kentrol dems bak te kee
en i sees dem, skwot en bisludgd op fra see
        rysing.
DEN dems happi.
ONLI dem dinna ken it . . .
DEMS nay ken wot dem in de wereld hev dun,
kos all bee onli intern in dem.
BUT i kennit.
    EN dems hidn happines shyn in mee!

/

FOR i ken eksistns ev de wereld.
Warefra kums dem hedfakts?
DEM kums fra ows skin.
SKIN smerts en skin gleems.
SKIN pulls us owt ev owselfs
  en twords udder menshis.
    ROBOTS nay be seprets
fra eech udder, dems nay bin born.
NAY skin seprets fra skin!
DEMS nay hav smerts nay hunge.
EN darefor nae hedfakts?

/

ROBOTS needs nay draums.

/

SUMTYMS wen sleepdraum i nay kan,
i draum e simpl, sili draum.
SO bee it: I imago mee
livs insyd en astroyd
wiv an hundrid udder menshis,
travls eway fra Sistm Sun
    nay mare muuns.
FOR all tym
onli travl owt.
  WIL dat lonli
in us den fershwins?
NAY poynt te get owt to
nay poynt te gang bak to.

NAY lengt mor.
LYK gots wil wee liv den,
drauming ev all
krying ovr na.

/

KUMS u wiv mee?

THE RAIN IN JANUARY

With a stupid bike I find myself
at a crossroads with no name
when you call
          about something wrong. Wrong
in the rain
where snow should have fallen
and the cones of light from a close car
should have swept past the roundabout's darkest grass
towards a home deep in the evening.
But everything bends inwards
in this rain that rains so wrong
against my glasses
and against the hospital mountain's
uppermost slope
I'm unable to see.
Does a rain exist there only
          for no one?
So gently the yellow bus glides
past the cement-mixing works
and the sign doorway's three
slip-roads! Like me, finally
on these reversed roads,
when you keep on saying
                    that Bente's not to come down again.
          But that only the rain is to come,
the rain that this evening rains so wrong
over every lamp post
and over this 'no'
I tie and tie

and that will probably
not ever come completely down.
  Now the image is separated from the image
and from a photo in your wallet
future flutters out of future
              absent-mindedly,
as if the world was just
a place in transit,
a forgotten shawl.
  For this the real has long since
given a promise about:
That everything will be turned back out again,
that everything will return
to streets with snow, dust
and sun with gleaming paint
in May, already August another year
and the features of a new face stand in the door
with such a strangely light nod
and a tricycle's split
hand-grip under the hedge
is now past recognition,
          unless the rain can do so,
which this evening probably only rains
as it once more will rain.

In memoriam Bente Gudmestad, 1968–2003

CAMOUFLAGE

On his newly stolen Kawasaki
our heroin-high neighbour also floats
          into the spring
that now rises
through the rose-hip bush's camouflage
we at this moment are thinking
we can vanish into,
as if seen with a cat's eyes drugged with sleep.
      Oblivion that's total
where the war's shattered soldier and an unsettled memory
can be borne away by a petal's
          sudden flash.
      On the verandah's
open bed we discuss the soul of the wasp
fighting in the wind
for its blind, unknown queen
and that therefore can never fly astray.
Oh, life in the perfect state!
      I gaze into
your black hair. A strand of silver
grows there. Is it growing
towards its ultimately
farthest out? Or is it just waiting
for its thousand sisters?
      Laburnum-gold, rhododendron-
pollen, 'Wild horses'
and the signal from a cell phone
that sends an arc in from a third
or fourth world (Ole?).

But here no one answers.
Here everything already exists.

In the Parminedes-
hour the hair grows
into the wasp, the wind
into the state and quietly
we hide ourselves in thought's vacuum.
    An image
that resembles an image
of a life. An image,
even with this smoke from the meat on the grill
that now glides past
and disappears like a kiss
towards the sky's
      limitless theft.

FROM THE TITAN GATE
Torild Wardenær

GODDESS REPORT III

I behave like a goddess, become involved in cosmic affairs, it does not pass unnoticed but I take the attacks as caresses, parry with myrtle, ash-root, with fist and knee and omnipotence float like nectar, drip from finger-tips. I carry the commonest attributes, one day apples – as many as I want – imported from Brazil – another day a titanium-light, collapsible sceptre of unknown origin, easily transportable and, to take the external characteristics first, I am walnut-coloured, green-eyed, lightly draped, am most often close to the throne, close to a stellium of extinguished suns. I am half-human, half-suffering, seriously flirting with the demigods or engrossed with the sea-salt, with the former Congo, with patching felt shoes, or quite simply taken up with being worshipped – by the elements, by the universe.

GODDESS REPORT VIII

I am now in the worldly realm, midway between the Middle Ages and the year 3000, it is a fine age, I am of high rank, clad in leather, ritual, narrow-shouldered, have control over the Armada and my leadership style is unlike the generals'; it is hesitating and vacillating. I take frequent breaks, open and close a red lacquered box fairly unmotivatedly, fumble with my keys, fumble with the main plan, rub away at a piece of light amber and allow myself to be distracted by the fact that Botticelli also bore himself stylishly, that he painted light exactly as it looked when it wedged itself in an atrium in his home town or twined itself in Flora's flower-bedecked hair – this light which has anticipated my age, which is completely unchanging. And I listen when the stories of the famous naval battles are told, of Atlas, of brute strength, of the time a grandchild's child ate up a whole plate of millet. I guard the instincts, gleaming flecks in the dark cosmos of the body, but everything in its own time, now I finally make a challenge, stand guard over us: ratio, ratio and ratio! There are so many helpers, stonemasons, weavers and laser engineers, I gather them round me, hand out camp-beds. Let us sleep under an open sky, let us celebrate midsummer together, let us be friends.

GODDESS REPORT IX

I roam the island looking for hares, beetles, birds and snakes. I want to be their humble friend, but they keep away. I myself am compelled to keep both in motion and motionless. The animals interest me, but first and foremost I am interested in this modest island anchored in the sea.

It does not claim its right to a first place in the oceans, or a secure link to the mainland. It floats, lazy and elongated, dreaming that animals perceive time as endless and that that is why it keeps us above the water, and that neither now nor later does it intend to distinguish between, for example, the hares and me.

POEM I

I look at this cherry tree as if it was the last thing I would ever do
I look at it with all the gravity I can muster in the face of a possibility which is not so infinitesimally small, at a point in June when
the leaves still glisten and the blossoms have budded into small green
berries, the wind is from the south, there is sunlight, though not too
sharp since it is covered by a layer of cloud; and I decide that this is
not to be a scientific observation where the focus is on leaf-nerves,
species and refraction, or an investigation of the extent to which the
cherry-tree bugs or insects from the gnawing of deer have attacked
them, but it's not pure contemplation as I don't intend to release the
object the moment it overwhelms me, which is what the cherry tree
always does, even though I haven't told myself to look at it as if it
was the last thing I was going to do, and the air is golden until the
day in June turns unannounced into November and I don't regret it,
do not try to stop the sudden change of season – even though it
starts with biting rain in addition to the sea-wind – since this is also
a fine time to look at the cherry tree, besides which I was born in
November, the month in which the branches are bare – one great
entangled declaration to us, i.e. me and my twin-soul, now we lead
each other round the tree in the cold wind, two bodies, two souls, it
crunches underfoot when we walk on the hill, which is covered with
cherry stones and twigs, and my twin-soul insists on leading me
round the tree as if it was a Christmas tree, she wants us to sing and
dance and even finally lie down next to the trunk, close together –
and the dark that branches over us will begin to blaze out of love
towards us, and the berries with their red flesh will swell in our
mouths.

POEM II

I look at this face as if it was the last thing I would ever do
and now it is in a way serious, since she is in a coma
the bed she is lying in is a vessel pitching in high seas
I follow along like a small sleek dolphin
singing inaudibly as dolphins do at a high, high frequency
for she is still breathing, raspingly but regularly, both thumbs folded
over her palms, her nose starting to turn blue, her toes white, her
eyes rolling
she is learning to make her own way, I'm not scared since I am a
dolphin following closely, we're in our element now, the sea is so
rough, the depths darkening beneath the depths and I will show
them to my twin-soul, but she has hidden herself away in the foliage
to build a secure winter lair, I smile indulgently, call her softly and
she comes, reluctantly, apprehensively, with hazel leaves in her hair
and seaweed under her nails, I get her to sit and soon we are gliding
together beside the ship and seen from the outside it all seems quite
inconspicuous, two twin-souls, one at each side of the bed in perfect
symmetry, along with the person dying.

POEM IV

492
357
816

I look at these numbers as if it was the last thing I would ever do and they hold me in a refined contemplation, perfectly suited to this act they look at me more than I do them, the dear familiar signs, the four, seven, three, eight, oh, I remember eight . . .
the memories are multiple and the numbers include me in their innermost accounts and they keep to their grid, to their fixed sum; promise me I'll be included in some way or other, even after death, when they continue to multiply or divide and I immediately want to tell my twin-soul this, but she is sitting fingering her own abacus, is humming, not sparing herself, squandering thoughts; both pre-occupied and calculating.

POEM V

I look at myself as if it was the last thing I would ever do
and I am just as predisposed now as when I was to look at, for
example, the cherry tree and the numbers, but this time I'm afraid it
may be more complicated since my body calls for so much attention
that I know that despite its relative lightness it constitutes an extra
dimension, huge and incalculable
my twin-soul has nothing to do with this, she stays discreetly in the
background, so everything takes place between me and my inner
organs and my skin, which winds sensually around my body,
unbroken, fragrant, holding the rest in place; my intestines, tuned
smooth by herbs and boiled water; my flesh, soft and sweet; and a
tearaway of a soul that forages between vertex and solar plexus at a
creditable rate.

I try to be both the mother and father of this system, also sizing
myself up to act as both its benefactor and spiritual head. This is by
no means an insurmountable challenge, I can see that from the facial
expressions of my twin-soul. She stays appreciatively at arm's
length, but has laid the warm palm of her hand against my back so
that I can lean back easily.

THIS IS WHERE I HAVE GOT TO, AND I EXPECT NOTHING

This is where I've got to, and I expect nothing
not happiness, not understanding eternity.
Only want to put out time and place's sinkers
breathe as long as is necessary
hold one formula after the other up to the light.
For the body has worn itself out again
is laden with grey matter, lime and gall
it floats on land and on water towards the world's borders and
hunger finally forces me to eat stars.
I eat them raw.
It is the seventh day, some still remain untouched in the firmament
a piece of Virgo and fortunately the whole Corona Borealis.
The consonants stand in their boxes, the numbers in their rows,
but all this is uncertain, electricity sparks along

the copper ways, in the magnesium pieces and the silver nodes and
we are stowaways.

I manage to stammer out: I love you.
The digested stars light up my stomach and parts of my pelvis.
I take you by the hand, cradle your head.
Are you blind, I ask, has death struck you blind?
I myself have almost been struck dumb from such travel.

AT ANY TIME AT ALL I CAN BE SEIZED
BY A SUDDEN MADNESS OF INFINITY

At any time at all I can be seized by a sudden madness of infinity and
also be possessed by all the lives that until now have been lost.
Possessed by the fact I myself have survived; by the days that
consume lovers;
by the incessant listening to the body's red interior.
I have gone mad, but am protected against the north wind and
surrounded by warnings.
My knee-caps are full of silver and serum. A master of the night
chants and a mummy
stands bending over me.
During the day her hair is covered by a cranberry-coloured scarf.
At night it hangs over my face while she watches over me, and it is
now while I lie like a novice and try out my future deathbed, it is
now in the short while it takes before she lights a lamp and it gleams
in an inlaid stone she wears in her ear, it is now that the warnings
take shape.
It is here in the zone between childhood and god's kingdom that she
gives a sign to the master of the night and giver of life, and the room
expands once more into a larger room where I shall wake up and fall
in love again, promise too much.

BREATHLESS, WITHOUT A SOUND

Breathless, without a sound but close as if you were here right now, your words mingle with my own fumbling signs, with my breath that continues as if nothing had happened.

If only I could revel in the silk-time, gently torn from real time, the hardest one, the one on which laws must be founded, the one that keeps us so sharply separated.

Your handwriting is here even so, the letters resemble the joys and tribulations of earthly life without naming a single embrace, without mentioning a single bitter complaint. Only elves flee from sign to sign, from mouth to finger-grip, and between the lines torn time stands chaste.

Day and night I read between the lines and err between the points of the compass, but not all the rites or prayers of the world will be able to recreate this time of innocence that has escaped our poor control, our shattered calendar.

We believe it will have to stand like this for ever, motionlessly and incomprehensibly consecrated above us, but it must hold us in a grip even though we are separate.

For the truth is that it is in its own cycle, recurrent, gleaming, already marked with letters – and at some time it will drift into a distant galactic trap and with the aid of the full force of our childlike hearts be slung back.

I PASS THROUGH THE RANKS OF THE LIVING
AND THE RANDOM ORDER OF THINGS

I pass through the ranks of the living and the random order of things.

First: egg, bulb, demarcation of wounds, the square roots of large numbers, frequent retreats from the sting of death, tweezers, stainless steel, Viking ships and an eternal common babble.

Then that which calls for greater devotion: the absent beloved and the syllable above all syllables, the holy sound OM.

Then comes the going through of the third, fourth and fifth orders and I cannot, hand on heart, say that I am getting increasingly sharpened. On the contrary, I am relapsing into wishful thinking, into believing that the paradisiac place is less than a month's march away or that grief will not last more than seven days. I cannot manage on my own to hold phenomena apart and summon a collective memory that perhaps knows more about the annihilation of the dinosaurs or the number ten to the hundredth.

And memory seeks, for everything is scattered, lost through history, military coups, the battle of Issos in 333, the battle of the Vadimos lake, the slave war, the battle of the Teutoburger forest in year nine, the first Punic War, the battle of Tannenberg, the Rule of Terror in 1793 – everything has to be picked up again, examined piece by piece, the ruined coats of mail, the rent skin, the crushed bones and all the blood, where it came from and where it ran to, streams of blood sucked into the ground among the now almost untraceable atoms from the soldiers' childhood lives, for example the mother's milk trickling from the gaping mouths of the small boy children, alternately suckling and staring in devotion at their young mothers – those who were decorated with glass beads and gold clasps.

Perhaps going through the order of things can only be set in motion by special astronomic events or by as yet unknown testing methods or via the courage and extraordinary sensitivity of the trial subjects. For it is difficult to prove what it means to be alive for a while. It can apparently not be done even under the most rigorously controlled conditions, and I must finally, with my usual scientific integrity, state that there is a final number, but that it is scarcely in one's power – as a perfectly ordinary mortal – to conjure it up.

CLUBS DAGGERS BROADSWORDS

. . . CLUBS DAGGERS CUTLASSES PICKAXES REVOLVERS
SULPHURIC ACID KNIVES AXES HALBERDS CYANIDE
BATONS SHEATH KNIVES SHOT CANNONS LANCES
RIFLES RAPIERS FLOATING MINES SABRES BAZOOKAS
FOILS MACHINE GUNS ATOM BOMBS CARBINES SICKLES
POISON GAS MUSKETS TORPEDOES SCIMITARS CATA-
PULTS NAPALM FLINTLOCKS HAND GRENADES AIR
GUNS DDT MAGNETIC MINES MITRAILLEUSES TANKS
STEN GUNS LONGBOWS MINES BLUNDERBUSSES MAUSERS

. . . glottis, leather skin, lymph nodes, capillary loops, lumbar
vertebrae, meniscus, synovial joints, cerebellum, glia cells, adrenal
cortex, Bowman's capsule, lunar bone, pupil, ureters, nasal septum,
occipital lobes, appendix, jugular arteries, cranial cavity, portal
vein, Merkel's disc, hymen, wisdom teeth, sublingual gland,
Cremaster muscle, lachrymal, sinusoidal node, ilium lumbar
muscle, iris, Eustachian tubes, anytenoid cartilage, mitral valve,
cuneiform bone, pericardium, ball joint, rib cartilage, parietal lobe,
arteries, tailor muscle, inner anklebone . . .

MUSTARD GAS HARPOONS FUSES LAND MINES SLEDGE-
HAMMERS NEUTRON BOMBS ARSENIC ARMOUR-
PIERCING SHELLS GUILLOTINES DEPTH CHARGES
HUNTING KNIVES SHRAPNEL MACHETES FLAME
THROWERS HYDROGEN BOMBS ANTI-AIRCRAFT GUNS
SALOON RIFLES CRUISE MISSILES NITRIC ACID CLUBS
BAYONETS TANKS STILETTOS BROADSWORDS SPEARS
STICKS SLINGS LANCETS SCALPELS NERVE GAS CLUSTER
BOMBS . . .

EVERY DAY THERE IS SOMEONE TO THANK

Every day there is someone to thank. Today: the eastern yogis, the wise women, the innumerable charismatic people and learned Europeans. To begin with, I certainly thank them for initiation into the problem of the infinite, but rather unexpectedly I can be assailed by doubt and disquiet. That they advance the infinite as a fundamental reality makes me feel both worried and euphoric. And on account of the diversity within which infinity is defined and everything it seems to demand of me, untrained as I am at thinking, I feel a tightening of the jaw, the skull and the pineal gland. Yes, even of the coccyx, os sacrum, the holy nodular bone feels sore when I am overwhelmed by the universe, the earth's axis, the night of genesis, the primeval substance, the life principle, eternal life, the sexual urge, mental power, etc. Everything coils so closely around me, like Ourobouros, the world serpent, and I am forced out of the house and set about cutting down a rose bush. The branches scratch me, get entangled in my clothes and hair. The root stands firm, but I work away for a long time with my pole to loosen it. I can see from the white root system that it has grown and thickened while I have been living here, but the summers have whirled past, have become intangible. The maltreated root gives off ethereal oils whose scent already grows weaker as I stand there. Is it true that the flowers it has nourished have been haunted by generations of butterflies, the very insect of metamorphosis itself, that hundreds of nuthatches have landed here, that the sound of the wind, falling snow and the birds chirp have taken place at the same time as wars far away have raged incessantly, and that in its time of growth millions have shifted from human life to nuclear particles, yes, that some of those closest to me have done precisely that?

Will there be traces of them here in this freshly uncovered white pith?

Everything artfully pursues me, like the elves in the forest go after those lost in the forest, like the cycle of the emperor moth is followed by the cycle of the emperor moth. The theories of infinity have driven me out of the house, I have been scratched, am sweating, drink several litres of water and for that reason become less dehydrated and also see an end to the speculations, but it is perhaps only a temporary relief, a kind of mild deception.

I AM EXPOSED TO THREATS

I am exposed to threats of excruciating emptiness
pressed up against a point of the compass, but
quickly break free, seek the forest floor where tormentil and moss
grow
where I find everything I need to eat: sweet, sour, salt, sharp and
bitter
find dashes of elf-blood on the stones, signs of battle, lovemaking
what has happened, I become so dizzy from these almost invisible
conspiracies,
of the liberalism and the not-unexpected abundance
from standing and staring beneath the heavy pine trees
from feathers and daisies and medicinal plants
from intersecting persuasions and fairytales and the owls, towhoo
the owls that have begun to speak my language.

I AM BEREFT OF REASON

I am bereft of reason, quite dark and not precisely begging to have
the pain, the gift that no one else wants either, but it is given to me
unasked, is wearing the heavy crown, carrying the unmistakable
sceptre that gleams so incomprehensibly. The casket, full of sharp
gems, is opened.

I am dealt stings, grazes and blows and the speckled train envelops
me, touches my chin, my shins, root of my nose and skull and I lie
down, for this is the pain, it comes with itself, is the gift of gifts, is
sometimes clad in regalia, is sometimes stiff and staccato like a
Prussian general, undeservedly decorated or

it comes undemanding, with a tunic on, wearing glasses and
speaking simply like the Dalai Lama,

but I do not understand anything even so, wriggle free

and the area between us is blocked off, all life is startled into flight
and I follow a

flight of birds with my eyes until I cannot see it any more, until the
sky swallows it and

my instincts cease.

I wallow in nightmares but do so quickly, like a winter bather,
harden myself, loosen my tongue, speak pidgin in the twilight,
forget my native language and allow myself to be dazzled by the
mysteries of words, by the outer appearance of things

for it is still light, though the dark is approaching, the forgotten
force, and I am alone although something else is always here, it is a
spirit that captures language or the central nervous system
or whatever other territory between us.

IN WRITING I MUST HAVE REVERSED THE NUMBERS

In writing I must have reversed the numbers and automatically and with a firm hand I have written 3002 instead of 2003. I simply take this as a sign that it will become true that we will be there together, on an April day a thousand years in the future.

I write April 3002. The magpies are kicking up a racket above the trees and roofs. The colour of the new grass is ancient, but it lays its young pigment round us. It is just after the great revolutions. We have survived and learned so much, how we can be interconnected, for example. We still risk there being light-years between us, but the distances will be overcome in the space of seconds and with the aid of clarity of thought and purity of the heart.

To be on the safe side I am therefore already conjuring both my and your atoms into a new incarnation, for I do not want to miss these future connections, the magpies' riotous play under the enormous spring sky, that the world will still be bursting with life.

FROM **PSI**
Torild Wardenær

INHERITANCE CCXCIV
UNSECURED I

Towards Sagittarius, 25,000 light years away, the young Pistol Star
reels around its own detonated mass, a hundred and fifty times
stronger than the sun, fully loaded, unsecured and out of the holster.
Not that I let myself be threatened, but lift my arms even so and
place myself against a wall
volunteer my personal details

kingdom: animalia
series: chordata
order: primata
family: hominidae
lineage: homo
species: sapiens
habitat: terrestrial and

late in the series of evolution, with epithelia and spine and circulatory organs fully grown and of an extraction partially unknown, partially Milanese, although I also admit to descent from chiton, turbellaria and flukes, that I belong to a highly developed species, but that I am not yet able to love my neighbour, admit that even my most unselfish acts can be counted on one hand, something the pale sky above me has disapprovingly been a witness to and behind me the Pistol Star fires away in all directions while I press myself up against a wall, showing my face as if it was a cosmic mark, as if it would grant me free passage.

INHERITANCE CCCVII
SECOND METAPHYSICAL EXCURSION

My comrades and I are holding up the world, athletically, hip to
hip, cranium to thumb,
navel to rib, pelvis to mouth, tooth to neck, mucous membrane to
nail, tongue to tongue,
forehead to sky – this sky again – from one direction there comes
ethnic music, men and
women are singing into old-fashioned microphones from a studio
in the Balkans, it jars on an
inexplicable wavelength, from another direction frost comes
slobbering, I look around for
some neutral witnesses, but there are none to be had and the sea
outside is a single constant
interference, I want to ask Mechthild von Magdeburg about
something, but she of course does not
answer, or says something in her unintelligible Plattdeutsch from
1279, so I'll have to work it out for
myself, look up, once again the sky seems to be quite treacherous,
not unexpectedly it mirrors the
unruly sea, I take out my small inspection mirror, still with its
splendour from the days of glory in Murano
and insert it between the projections, edges, scars here in the small
section of the world clinic, full of
wound sites, try to put something together of scissors, sex, subject
and septet, all gleaming, distinct
elements and said quickly and in any order at all they call for
action, keen
action – or perhaps just to continue reliably holding up the world,
shoulder to shoulder with my
comrades, or how about leaving the whole thing to Atlas and a

host of gods once more, for if we let
go, other constructions are waiting behind the facades of the
senses.

INHERITANCE CCCXXVI
FIFTH METAPHYSICAL EXCURSION

Time passes noisily above me, I stand underneath, half safe, half in
danger and have forgotten how
I got from Almeria to Mojacar, have forgotten the time of day and
individual circumstances
concerning the journey.
Was it in August or May, was it in the morning or the afternoon,
and who received me,
if anyone did.
Did I eat a papaya or an orange in the sweltering bus.
Did I peel the fruit with the attention and care it deserved.
Was there some pith there, between the peel and the flesh that I
neglected – a white or waxlike
membrane, immediately exposed to the greedy Mediterranean
light, to inevitable oxidation?
Was there a little invalid boy there, at the front of the bus, along
with his relative?

And if any shipwreck dramatically took place off the rugged coast
right then because I passed, no,
not on account of me, but despite my secretiveness, my need of
meaning, my eternal
circumpolar ego, was it not as if stars and satellites would follow
me with their
controlling gaze, as if the coast would hold me out against the
horizon and show me to a
death struggle where none of those drowning would have any
future memory of me – or, I am mistaken;
death is holding out continent upon continent for all those
drowning, just like dry land would

hold a traveller or survivor out towards the sea, towards the
unfathomable amounts of water
that have children and women and sailors and sunken cities on
their conscience. Conscience?
I bite my tongue, dissatisfied with my choice of word, am already
sharpened, am already abandoned to
a focal point of forgetting there, in the shelter of the bus, without
air conditioning but servo-controlled,
that passes the plantations with tomatoes and avocados and all
sorts of crops as if I were a
moving focus, as if I was the gaze of a shaman instead of my own
strange
introverted one, and why else am I so desirous of people; the little
invalid with
a piercing voice, the farmers out there on the green plateaus, a
wife's complaint and quick,
loud account of the absolutely basic *casa, muerte, amor*, her fellow-
travellers
listening with only half an ear, he takes no notice of her fiery
gestures, he is looking at my light skin, but
I am already lost to this moment, to the world, for ever.

I burst into tears, unintentionally, but also to ensure that via this
unsuitable
reaction I will one day feature, far away and in ghostlike fashion, in
someone's
confused memory.

INHERITANCE CCCXXVII
I AM FIXING MY KARMA

I am fixing my karma, travelling around Europe exchanging words
for reality – a little salted butter
for some T-rays or gamma rays or radio waves and I'm standing in
a barter economy, in
the radiance – half self-sufficient, half beggar, and dry land and
ocean spread out distinctly
and dispassionately from me and everything seems to be
independent of my existence; pitching
ships loaded with iron and turbines, oil installations, erosion of
coral reefs and the awe-inspiring life
of the moray eels, and I do not take it personally that the sea
growls and sends me packing
over the Baltic with *M/S Georg Ots* or that there is singing on
board, of summer nights on
Saarimaa and the girl with flaxen hair and her Karelian cousin, the
song sets everything in motion:
the accordionists, the dancers, the ship that bears the singer's name
and the song is about some
notorious lovers in another century, they have long since been
fused on to sepia-brown paper where a
crossfire from the bridegroom's brain sent a splinter into his left
eye, an evening prayer to his right and
in her gaze no childbed fever, cold and hunger are depicted but
whole consummations, like
the inside of glistening seeds and in her arms she holds the largest
garden flowers cultivated in the
region, they grew and grew under the sun, but I have no possibility
of keeping the past at arm's length

or the moment intact for the vessel is making good speed and to
the east an extended forest-clad island is in sight, to the west the
unbridled oceans are raging and the ship lingers long by the coast, I
see a single house in the forest, it joins me like the island to the sea,
like the sea to the ship, like the ship to its destination, like the
captain to his instruments, like the town ahead to the cobbles and
arches
and the earth is not flat, but I do not heave a sigh of relief for that
because it curves around me,
squeezes me between a rusty container port and St Nicolas'
Church, mashes out of me
my last coins and a partial vacuum spreads me among people and
pastures but the words gather
me up, put me together, they gleam like mica or genuine money
and I give them away
again, almost for free, for it is economic theory and quantum
mechanics that will finally
explain me and pay me back to world circulation.

INHERITANCE CCCXXIX
THIRD LONELINESS TRIAL

I let go while the years rock and the stars fall and the sweet pea
seeds first sprout then flower
and wither from petal to dust and remain lying between the pages
of edifying books: Søren Kierkegaard's *Works of Love* and Werner
Spalteholz's *Hand Atlas of Human Anatomy* – pale bookmarks
between the living and the dead

and a single two-stroke engine continues to gently chug through
the summer or is it Mendel's
laws of succession that carry us deep into a future that shapes itself
partly according to us and partly as
it sees fit and I cannot prevent more time from surging in and
burying us
as we are once more drinking from the same bowl and you are
gone for good while I appear to be
alive, break off a piece of time as if nothing had happened, hold it
between
my hands for a moment before suddenly losing it deep down a
world cleft, but
I am already sure that it is not lost for ever
I am already sure that archaeologists or moles will protect it.

INHERITANCE CCCXXX
FIELD STUDIES II

The seaward approach calm and without engines across green lakes
with mountains that descend into
the water and Jalapeño birds in flight over them – how can I
explain this: every morning to get a new
watermark when arriving at field I from field II, these areas not so
dissimilar, but often
this journeying between them describes some strange distances
along the dark mountains, beneath
the hunting birds and in this demotorised sailing trip from the
particular exactness of sleep, an
ecstasy that can only be measured in its own ecstasy and in the firm
admission of the sin of the waking
world and in the great initiations that have to be counted on every
night – all this in the greatest intimacy
and exactitude along with some outburst or other from animals or
humans in distress or joy, the
scraping of claws against an underlying surface, water in motion,
the rattling of strange ceremonies and
customs, the war in progress, the almost soundless cardinal fish,
the whoosh of the closest fixed stars.

What can I say about this simultaneity that blends with the sharp
cries from the
hunting Jalapeño birds?
A moment of absolute pitch is unexpectedly granted me and
naturally I seize the opportunity,
identify the note precisely in the transition between field I and field
II and say:
'That is a C sharp.'

INHERITANCE CCCXXXII
TO XENA, MY DESCENDANT

Glands and stars seem not to be synchronised, for the years
stumble after each other
or fall into a coma and I fear that we have not lived and that
nothing has happened, that what we
hold up between before and now, no matter how visible and
tangible, will not lead to, that an
unexpected but simple solution will wind both itself and us out of
chaos and into a gleaming meantime

but these are insignificant remarks, for you are to take over the
future, an unharmed
survivor, you are to bear my genes and for the time being I call you
simply Xena after the newly
discovered heavenly body close to Pluto, the outermost planet
which after the discussions of The
International Astronomical Union can come to lose its status and
be banished to
the Kuyper Belt – perhaps precisely on account of Xena, methane-
beautiful and named after
a warrior princess, but it is certain that Pluto will continue to
transmit its diffuse light towards your
iris and perhaps it is particularly the gaze, along with the ears or
the form of the cranium that will be
the only recognisable feature left after so many generations, but
you will probably not even know what the weight of a past is, for
the fifth, sixth and seventh dimension will probably have been
taken care of by then, and whether you know or not, you are to
bear my genes, be an ambassador or vagrant in the new world

all this I am familiar with, *you* I am already familiar with.

INHERITANCE CCCXXXIII
PSI = ✕ (Ψ +10^{100})

Give me a P! Preferably Pluto with its moons of night and
underworld, Charon, Nix and Hydra, and if everything goes
according to plan, the New Horizon probe, which will arrive on a
peaceful mission in 2015.
Give me an S! The Sombrero galaxy decorated with infrared light.
Give me an I! Isis and Osiris, Inanna and Dumuzi

Give me anything at all – preferably seeds that have survived the
winter in astronomical numbers and
that precisely now are turning in the soil while I am appointed to
live on, in a cosmological
golden age, surrounded by everything and
I subscribe to the three known dimensions, but am constantly
chasing new formulas, sometimes
with the inspection mirror held up high, at other times it lies
forgotten in a deep-sea cleft and
gleams blackly for an eternity, and even though time occasionally
haunts me clad in a train of Goya's
winged monsters or quite simply passes by, loaded down with
medals meant for the murky heads of
state of this world, I normally steer it into a newly established
colony or let it roam around
among its own four-dimensional hiding places and
another field – this one; close, as we have always believed, but now
it presents itself
just as effortlessly as a sunrise, attracted by the hissing of its own
name

psi = the fifth dimension where everything is allied and never gets
lost
psi = the subatom – powerful and reserved at one and the same
time
psi = Ψ, the 23rd letter in the Greek alphabet
psi = the wave that causes the sky and the earth to change places
voluntarily

So? We all know this and always have.
May it just take over us and change us, may it just be of use to us.

INHERITANCE CCCXXXIV
WORKS OF LOVE IV

Struck once more by a rare high-frequency sound, inaudible as if
from dog whistles or just inaudible with
a distinct aura, as if from a strange sound faculty that splinters all
known megahertz
and spreads out that also the innermost archives, also that which
world history does not mention
exists in a distant pulsar or in an overgrown sector somewhere, in
some walls and

everything sinks and rises at the same time, keeps the visible in
check, keeps the inexhaustibility of the
invisible possible right in the world and a sudden agreement
between us to inherit
each other alive, to mix luminous cells now, steel and unknown
goods from the holy
future do not only apply to us two among other lovers – no,
everything is included: stones and
plants and animals stand in the same testamentary guild, also those
who have been disinherited,
whether they know it or not, whether they want it or not, and

we are to inherit each other, not on account of a sudden, rare high-
frequency sound, not
as a result of the doubtful mandate of this poem, but to inherit each
other in reality, in a truly
revolutionary and romantic act that admittedly may appear
ridiculous on a sober
day as this – but we know better.

ABOUT THE AUTHORS

KJARTAN FLØGSTAD

Kjartan Fløgstad (born 1944) is widely regarded as one of the most important and influential Norwegian writers today. Since his literary debut in 1968, he has written eight novels, several collections of poetry, essays, thrillers, short stories, travelogues, plays and non-fiction. In 1977 he was awarded the Nordic Council's Prize for *Dalen Portland*, his international breakthrough. *World Literature Today* claims: 'Kjartan Fløgstad has a playful creative temper and is a spirited prose writer virtuoso, delighting in aphorisms, parody and bizarre humour. Behind this, however, stands a mordant social critic.'

His novels always demonstrate a global awareness and a strong sense of solidarity with the oppressed. He exposes the forces that have shaped industrial and post-industrial society, and believes that a wealth of knowledge and indispensable strategies for a meaningful existence can be found in different forms of popular culture, both traditional and modern. *Fyr og flamme* (Fire and flames, 1980), *U3* (1983), *Det syvende klima* (The seventh climate, 1986) and *Kron og mynt. Eit veddemål* (Heads or tails. A wager, 1998) are his most important novels, while *Sudamericana 2000* represents his excellent travel writing. Fløgstad has won several awards, among them the Critics' Prize 1980, the Brage Prize 1998, and Medalla de Honor Presidencial Internacional Centenario Pablo Neruda 2004.

Recent publications are *Paradise on Earth* (2002), *Grand Manila* (2007) and *The Pyramid, a Portrait of a lost Utopia. Essays* (2007).

Fløgstad's writing is translated into several languages, including English, German, French, Spanish and Russian.

JOHAN HARSTAD

Johan Harstad (born 1979) offers a wholly original voice, seeing human fates in modern reality in a way that is both urgent and refined, offering a complete involvement and a particular sense of absurd humour. His characters often stand slightly to one side, at a distance from the major pulse of society. They are vulnerable, lonely, different.

In his first novel, *Buzz Aldrin, what happened to you in all the confusion?* (2005), Harstad tackled the big questions: What does it mean to be a human today? What is important in our lives? The narrative voice is convincing, and the protagonist Mattias strives to be the invisible second man, the cog, the one nobody notices. A grand-scale novel about life, sea, death and love, it references popular culture, lyrics, songs and bands. '*Buzz Aldrin* is an enchanting adventure with a terrifically good narrator' (*Het Patrool*, Amsterdam).

Hässelby (2007) is about a minor disaster that strikes the Stockholm suburb of Hässelby in the summer of 1983. It focuses on Albert Åberg and his father, who does the best he can and still ends up a helpless idiot.

Johan Harstad made his debut in 2000 aged 21, with a contribution to *Postboks 6860*. He published his first collection of prose works, *From here on you just get older*, in 2001, followed by a collection of short stories, *Ambulance*, in 2002. He has also written two pieces for the theatre, the first a monologue, *Degrees of White*, and the second a one-act play, *Washington*.

Harstad's work has been translated into Danish, Swedish, Finnish, Russian, Faroese, German, Dutch, French, Italian, English and Korean.

TORE RENBERG

Tore Renberg (born 1972) made his literary debut in 1995 with the collection of short prose *Sleeping Tangle*, for which he won the prestigious Tarjei Vesaas' Debutant Prize. He has published several novels and children's books, one collection of prose and one book of collages. His novel *I Loved Them All* was well received in Norway and Sweden; it has been filmed and is due for release in Norwegian cinemas in 2008. His novel *The Orheim Company* was nominated for the 2005 Brage Prize for Best Norwegian Novel.

During the 1990s Renberg distinguished himself as a literary critic, working for the literary magazine *Vagant* and hosting the programme *Leseforeningen* on the Norwegian Broadcasting Corporation. In 2004 he wrote his first film script *Alt for Egil*. Renberg is also a musician, and currently plays in the band Modan Garu.

'One of the most interesting authors to have emerged since 2000. He is a brilliant storyteller with a remarkable language and an original voice' (*Tønsbergs Blad*).

Praise for *The Orheim Company*:

'A page-turner, well told and well constructed . . . exceeding all expectations . . . Renberg's best. We will be waiting impatiently for the third book about Jarle' (*Stavanger Aftenblad*)

'An entertaining and inviting novel, which also offers insights about what being human entails' (*Norwegian Broadcasting Corporation*)

'Touchingly emphatic . . . well-written, and more than a little intelligent' (*Dagens Næringsliv*)

'Believable, gripping and essential . . . Renberg has found his *force*, which is the personal narrative . . . an important book' (*Klassekampen*)

'Renberg reaffirms his strength as a writer . . . He is an expert at building characters . . . will attract many readers' (*Dagbladet*)

'Renberg continues his exploration of the vulnerability and exposure attached to growing up in a world that does not always agree with one's expectations. The novel distinguishes itself with a good insight into human relations. The main character is portrayed with tenderness and sensitivity, and has become a distinct and authentic figure in Norwegian contemporary literature' (Jury recommendation, Brage Prize nomination)

SIGMUND JENSEN

Sigmund Jensen (born 1968) is regarded as one of his generation's most prolific, significant and interesting voices. Since his debut in 1995 with *Antikvarens datter og andre noveller* (The Antiquarian's daughter and other stories), he has published two more story collections, *Motvilje* (Antipathy, 1998) and *Gammaglimt* (Gamma glimpse, 2004), all of which have been highly praised by critics.

A central theme in his work is lack of communication. His inspiration is apparently everyday life and situations, but in his latest collection Jensen has developed an imaginary yet recognisable universe, in which he approaches the human condition and ontological and existential questions. Jensen is best known for his novel *Hvite dverger. Svarte hull* (White dwarves. Black holes, 2002).

Jensen has been awarded the Aschehoug First Book Award (1995), the annual Rogaland County Literary Award (1999) and the Mads Wiel Nygård Award (2004). He is represented with short stories in several anthologies in Norway, Serbia, the Czech Republic, Poland and Hungary. One story has been adapted for the stage and performed by students in Budapest. One has been published in French by *Nouvelle Revue Française*. Jensen's second novel, *Tiberiusklippen* (The Tiberian cliff) is due in 2008.

Praise for *Hvite dverger. Svarte hull* (White dwarves. Black holes):

'Norwegian literature has found its own Peter Høeg . . . Sigmund Jensen's first novel is just as promising as Peter Høeg's decisive breakthrough' (*Weekendavisen*)

'It has been a long time since I read a Norwegian novel with such a high level of ambition . . . and such literary power and resilience' (*Dag og Tid*)

'Linguistically speaking, Jensen's elegant style has no match' (*Fædrelandsvennen*)

'Inventive and imaginative' (*Dagbladet*)

'Originally composed, sparkling, well-written . . . a new first-class novelist' (*Aftenposten*)

EINAR O. RISA

Einar O. Risa was born and still lives in the rural part of the Stavanger region. After studying literature, history and law, he started work as a journalist.

Risa made his debut in 1995, and has published several novels, all highly acclaimed in Norway. A strong fascination for the Norwegian writer Alexander L. Kielland (1846–1906) has led him to publish several books on the subject, including *Mannen i speilet – om Alexander L. Kielland i Stavanger* (1999).

Risa's individuality as a writer is linked to his precise descriptions, stripped-down and suggestive language and unique ability to interweave history, international politics and the lives of individuals. In 2000 he was awarded the Tiden Prize and in 2003 the Nota Bene Prize for his novel *L. C. Nielsens papirer.*

Risa's published novels are: *Skygger* (1995), *Ring* (1996), *Velvære* (1997), *Nasjonaldagen* (1998), *Helvete* (1999), *L. C. Nielsens papirer* (2000), *Casanovas siste erobring* (2002), *Likeså, skulle han si* (2003), *Kom, kom, hør nattergalen* (2005) and *Jeg går ikke ut lenger, jeg svever over byen* (2006).

ØYVIND RIMBEREID

Øyvind Rimbereid (born 1966) made his debut in 1993 with a collection of short stories *Det har begynt* (It has begun), followed by a novel (1996) and a second collection of short stories (1998). He has also published three poetry collections, which represent a major development in his work. While Rimbereid's prose is written in a realistic and modernistic literary tradition, his poetry can best be characterised as 'combinatory': he writes both short and long poems, epics, poems with a contemporary and historical content, and poems that are both personal and collective. In *Seine topografier* (Late topographies, 2000), his theme is his background in Stavanger. In *Trådreiser* (Following the threads, 2001) he embarks on factual and poetic travel in the margins of Europe, including north-west Russia and Scotland.

In his latest collection of poetry, *Solaris korrigert* (Solaris corrected, 2004), Rimbereid looks into the future and the year 2480. The long, epic poem describes Norway as a late-technology society, and is written in a hybrid language of West Norwegian dialect, earlier forms of Norwegian and elements of other languages from around the North Sea. In 2007, it was selected by a jury of critics, academics and writers as one of the 25 best Norwegian books of the year. In 2006 Rimbereid published a collection of essays, *Hvorfor ensomt leve?* (Why live in solitude?)

Rimbereid has been awarded several prizes, among them the Sult-prize (2001) and the Norwegian Critics' Prize for Literature (2005). A selection of his poetry has been translated into several European languages.

TORILD WARDENÆR

Torild Wardenær (born 1951) made her debut collection of poetry in 1994, followed by five further notable collections. In 1998 she made her debut as a dramatist with two short plays at the Norwegian Dramatists' Festival and at Rogaland Theatre's Theatre Workshop. She has also written a number of one-act plays and a play for children for Theatre Ibsen in 1999.

Wardenær has translated American and English poetry, worked as a critic for *Stavanger Aftenblad* and *Klassekampen*, has been a teacher and lecturer, and has been engaged in many cooperative projects with artists and musicians. She has had numerous articles published in Norwegian and international literary magazines and anthologies, and has written texts for photographic exhibitions, art installations and musical events. Her literary output includes drama, stage productions, essays, adult fiction, lyric poetry and translation. She has received a number of prizes, notably Herman Wildenvey's poetry award and the Halldis Moren Vesaas prize. Her latest collection of poems, *psi* (2007), has been highly acclaimed by Norwegain critics and has been nominated for the Brage Prize.

Wardenær's published collections of poetry are: *I pionértiden* (1994), *null komma to lux* (1995), *Houdini til minne* (1997), *Døgndrift* (1998), *Titanporten* (2001) and *Paradiseffekten* (The Paradise effect, 2004). The poems in the last-named collection present an aspect of the phenomenon of the title, 'the Paradise effect', in which the main character experiences all the multitude of details in the world, which overflow and threaten to overwhelm us, and must discover and concentrate on the elements that really deserve attention.

Praise for *Paradiseffekten*:

'A brave, thought-provoking and well-accomplished poetry collection' (*VG*)

'It is a pleasure to read Wardenær's long, rhythmic, sensual sentences' (*Aftenposten*)